Eve's Tattoo

Clea and Zeus Divorce

*A Visit from the Footbinder
and Other Stories*

World War II Resistance Stories

*The Official I-Hate-Videogames
Handbook*

Roger Fishbite

Roger Fishbite

A NOVEL

EMILY PRAGER

RANDOM HOUSE

NEW YORK

Library of Congress Cataloging-in-Publication Data
Prager, Emily.
    Roger Fishbite : a novel / Emily Prager. – 1st ed.
        p.   cm.
    ISBN 0-679-41053-8
    I. Title.
PS3566.R25R64   1999
813' .54–dc21   98-24408

Random House website address: www.atrandom.com
Printed in the United States of America on acid-free paper
2 4 6 8 9 7 5 3
First Edition
Book design by Victoria Wong

Roger Fishbite

A NOVEL

EMILY PRAGER

RANDOM HOUSE

NEW YORK

Copyright © 1999 by Emily Prager

All rights reserved under International and Pan-American Copyright Conventions. Published in the United States by Random House, Inc., New York, and simultaneously in Canada by Random House of Canada Limited, Toronto.

Random House and colophon are registered trademarks of Random House, Inc.

Library of Congress Cataloging-in-Publication Data
Prager, Emily.
    Roger Fishbite : a novel / Emily Prager. – 1st ed.
       p.   cm.
    ISBN 0-679-41053-8
    I. Title.
    PS3566.R25R64   1999
    813' .54–dc21   98-24408

Random House website address: www.atrandom.com
Printed in the United States of America on acid-free paper
2 4 6 8 9 7 5 3
First Edition
Book design by Victoria Wong

To all the little girls I've met who started out in desperate circumstances. It is their boundless determination and unstoppable joy in life that profoundly influenced this book.

The greatest honor is having you for a daughter.

–The father in Disney's *Mulan* (1998)

Acknowledgments

With thanks to my editor, Bob Loomis; my agents, Andrew Wylie, Sarah Chalfant, and Jin Auh; and especially to my family, Neke, Lulu, Mingus, and Stella.

Part One

1 "A pervert," my friend Eglantine said when she came to visit me in the holding cell. "You were involved with a pervert. Why didn't you tell me? What was he like?"

Serious, she cocked her head, listening for my answer. "Nervous," I replied. "His skin was as thin as old church parchment."

"And was there sex?" she asked, scrunching up her eyes and pushing down the thrill of asking me. I smiled at her in such a way that she would remember this moment all her life. Then I yawned with boredom.

"Yes," I said impatiently. "Yes, of course there was sex."

2 I called him Roger Fishbite right away. Right from that first minute that I answered the door and took him down to see the basement apartment. His mouth was big and turned down like a fish and he was huge and rather attractive. And like a fish, he didn't look dangerous. He didn't look like he would bite.

No, he looked just like my father, if the truth be told: six foot two, blond and pillowy—it took my breath away—he had that Texan warmth. But he had a fisheye, too, which suddenly stared at me, cold, unblinking, when my mother walked out of earshot into the kitchen, thinking he was following.

"Stop looking at me," I hissed at him.

"Yes, mistress," he replied and lumbered away after my mother.

I was twelve and a half years old and I was nobody's mistress. People called me miss and little miss and princess and Lucky Lady, which was the name on my birth certificate, but nobody ever called me mistress.

"What do you mean?" I called after him. "Like Mistress Mary Quite Contrary or a married man's girlfriend?"

But he didn't answer and I didn't expect him to. The way he said it, I was supposed to puzzle it out. It didn't sound mean, though, but like I was more grown-up than him, which I liked. But it was something he should not have said, which I picked up right away because I was not born yesterday, as my mother used to say, but almost. And he was certainly a weirdo.

He was not the first grown-up who liked me. They always did. Once, in second grade, when I was trick-or-treating, a grown-up opened the door, looked at me, and kissed me on the lips and shut the door back up before I even knew it. I was dressed as a private detective and I looked very sophisticated, much older than I usually did, which must have fooled him. I got my costume from a movie I saw on TV with Veronica Lake, who I like very much. I admire her slowness. She's careful and precise and slow like honey. On the outside, I seem like that. But on the inside, I'm a nervous child and I need to move fast. And that's just the way it has to be.

There were others: Mr. Lewis, who was the janitor of our apartment complex when we lived in Texas and my father was an intern. Mr. Lewis sat inside his tiny house in a stuffed armchair in front of a big TV and he drank buttermilk. He taught me that you could learn from watching television, learn all about the country, he said. High culture, low culture, it's all there for the taking. I don't remember what he looked like or anything else at all. And you know what's funny? I hate buttermilk.

And there was Rosalita's boyfriend, Senor Luxe. Rosalita lived in the complex too. She was big and blond with deep red lips, and when I visited her, which I did often, to try on her high heels and learn to walk in them, Senor Luxe would take my picture.

"Hand on hip," he would cry in his funny accent and then, as he looked through the lens, he'd mutter "*Ay caramba*" to himself.

I was "*linda*" in high heels, he said, "something else for four and a half," which made me proud, I have to say.

"What else?" I asked him once, but he just sweated.

Rosalita was very nice about her shoes. She didn't mind me playing there, although my mother wouldn't have liked it had she known. My mother thought I was at Mr. Lewis's, who she liked. Rosalita, she said, was a prostitute, a term I did not understand until recently, when I realized that she was probably right. Rosalita did have many boyfriends, but Senor Luxe was the only one I cared for.

And there were other grown-ups, I know it. I just can't remember them now, but I will if I keep thinking. They come to mind like butterflies, these tiny wisps of memory.

3

Dear Readers and Watchers of tabloid TV and press, I want you to know the truth. The water was gray, the deep gray of wet stones by a Chinese lake, a gray you couldn't see through. Sometimes the water was so dark, it was like a blackboard at school. Some children find it scary, not being able to see what's underneath, but I find it comforting. And you must judge, if I jumped in that water and a fish bit me, could it be my fault? Could it be? If I couldn't see the fish coming?

4

I was born Lucky Lady Linderhof, fifteen years ago tomorrow in Germaine, Texas, just outside of Dallas. My mother and father both came from Germaine. My mother was the daughter of a wildcatter who struck oil under the swing set in the backyard when she was fifteen and got rich. He lost it all again when she turned eighteen, and after that my mother had all her shoes dyed to match, no matter what the outfit. To me, she looked like Snow White the morning after, but once, when she was wearing a miniskirt on Broadway in summer, a man shouted at her, "Brooke Shields didn't get it all," which I also think sums her up.

Was she warm? a psychiatrist at the facility asked me just after they brought me in. And I had to tell him, I'm not old enough to answer that question. Can I still feel the shape of her hand? Can I still smell the heat of her skin? Yes, sir. I can.

My father, Tex Linderhof, was a legend in Germaine. He was a great football player, and the son of Germaine's doctor, Boop Linderhof. Tex went on to study medicine himself at Galveston and became an expert in cholera. He lives now in Pakistan and treats dying babies, which I'm sure makes him sad. He always loved kids, one of Boop's neighbors told a reporter after it happened, which makes what I did seem even more inexplicable. Did I mention he was Prom King?

I haven't seen or heard from Tex since he left my mother when I was four. Though that's not that unusual in American families, I agree with Geraldo Rivera when he says something should be done about it.

Did his leaving have something to do with what happened? Was I a daddy's girl in search of a daddy? Could it be as simple as that? How did I feel when I realized he was gone, so long ago, back, back, in my baby way? I couldn't understand where he had gone. I could not grasp why things were not the way they had been. And where he'd gone and what that meant. And the confusion was so deep and so all over me, it was like a witch's cloak. And for a long time I behaved like a witch. And then, after another year, which was a quarter of my life then, don't forget, I got over it.

5

My mother let the apartment to Roger Fishbite because he had "cash on the line" and he was my father's ex-brother-in-law, which I think made her feel like she was in touch with my father again. I knew he was going to be a pain but I didn't tell her. She needed the money for her lunchtime peels, and he did make me laugh.

He moved in on July 25, 1996, the day I learned that the life of a supermodel is not all glamour and fun. There was a conversation on MTV hosted by Cindy Crawford and all the models were complaining. I told Fishbite about it while he carried in his stuff.

"I don't know if I believe it," I said. "They make quite a bit of money and travel and are thoroughly lionized."

He stopped and stared at me. "How do you know a word like 'lionized'?" he asked suspiciously.

"Private school." I hissed this last, knowing he would like it, and he did.

"Anyway," I continued, "do you think the life of a super-model is all that bad?"

"You could model," he replied, stuttering, and hurried out the door, back to the moving van. I followed him out.

"I don't think I could model," I said. "I'm too thin."

He looked at me, surprised. He had blond hair and wore big, square glasses like from a French sixties movie which magnified his fishy eyes. Though he clearly thought other-wise, he did not have movie-star looks.

"You're too thin?" he repeated in disbelief.

"Yes. You need some meat on your bones to model these days. At this point, I'm just a stick. Look."

He gave me the once-over and his head shook. Then he rolled his eyes around in his head.

"What's the matter?" I asked. He was definitely behaving oddly.

"Nothing." He cleared his throat. "Nothing. The strain."

He nodded toward the objects he was carrying into the house, which I decided to take an interest in.

There was nothing in his possessions that would indicate the lengths to which he would finally go, the ends to which he would drive me. Except of course the typewriter on which he wrote down his stories, the stories the paper said later he couldn't sell.

Otherwise it was standard male-person stuff: a deco armchair, an old standing lamp, a double bed, a leather couch, a rolltop desk, a swivel desk chair, a small box of well-worn paperbacks—the trappings, now that I looked at them, of a private detective.

"Are you a gumshoe?" I asked him.

"A gumshoe," he repeated.

He was carrying boxes and boxes of what he said were books but could have been files into the apartment.

"You mean a detective?"

I nodded, closing my eyes like they do in the movies to indicate trustworthiness.

"No," he replied. "I'm a novelist."

"Lucky!" My mother came down the front stoop wearing one of those satiny dresses that looks like a slip and costs the earth. She got her clothes free from one of her friends who was a designer on Seventh Avenue and gay. I know from Oprah that a lot of men are gay who don't tell you. But my mother's friend told me right away when I first met him.

"I'm gay, which is lucky for you. What a cutie!" he exclaimed. "She looks just like a blond Snow White."

"Are you gay?" I asked Fishbite as my mother reached the bottom step. I could see she liked him. I thought she should know right up front.

He got pretty upset.

"Lucky!" my mother shouted.

"Well, you're moving into our house," I pointed out. "Two women alone. We are entitled to know what we're up against. Are you?"

I walked right up to him and put my face close to his so I could look right into his eyes and see his soul.

"No," he snapped, and stalked off toward the moving van. My mother gestured to me thumbs up. She'd trust a snake if it used hair mousse. According to Oprah, a lot of women would.

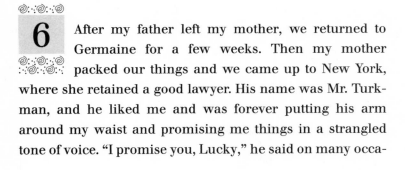

6 After my father left my mother, we returned to Germaine for a few weeks. Then my mother packed our things and we came up to New York, where she retained a good lawyer. His name was Mr. Turkman, and he liked me and was forever putting his arm around my waist and promising me things in a strangled tone of voice. "I promise you, Lucky," he said on many occasions, "that you will lead the life of a princess, as you are entitled," which always made my mother weep. But he never got any more money out of Tex. My mother adored Mr. Turkman and may have slept with him.

I didn't know that then, of course. The life of a young child, which some of you may not realize, is really a series of hindsights. It's all a frustrating blur until one day your brain is ready, and then (and to my knowledge they have not covered this on the talk shows) you suddenly can see so clearly, and you say Ohhhhh, so that's how you make Jack jump out of the box, so that's how you turn the handle, how you make your fingers grasp the piece of wood. I can do it! Let me do it again. And again.

It was like this, for me, with the following idea:

Just now, after some months here at the facility, I see that there exists a kind of grown-up man, his age between twenty-eight and ninety, who reveals himself to certain young girls painfully and utterly. He is the nice photographer, the friendly pastor, the jocular uncle, the mother's boyfriend, those whom the old books call "dirty old men."

Those who are younger than twenty-eight are simply disturbed. Those who are older than ninety are simply confused and can no longer find a difference between a twelve- and a twenty-five-year-old, so far away are they from the nuances of youth.

Is every man a dirty old man? Oh No! Were that true, then little girls would have no rest and certainly go mad. No, this is a special man, a man for whom a Catholic school uniform, even on a mannequin, does more than a whole album of grown-up girl nudes. A man whom Carter's white underpants titillate worlds beyond the classiest catalogue of frilly lingerie. A man whose knees, at the sight of a training bra on a flat chest, shake like Jell-O.

You can recognize such men only if you are or have been that Carter's-wearing girl. They do not have looks in common. There is no body type that gives them away. Just a certain nervous obsessiveness about their manner that only an expert would notice. That and the comfort they feel with little girls. No distance of age separates them; indeed, they seem not to notice age at all. Often you can find them on their knees before a child for no other reason than that they so wish to be the same height.

If you look at a photo of, say, the squash team of an elite athletic club, only a girl like me could pick out the one man who would love to take me rowing and snap pictures, the one man who would rather go with me to a department store children's section and shop than to a sports game, the one man over whom I have, as such a man once wrote, "fantastic power."

Did I forget a sense of humor? They always have one. Did I forget betrayal? It always follows. I read *Faust* at school, and they're the devil. And do you think, Readers and Watchers, that I sold my soul to Fishbite? The New York Department of Correction, Juvenile Division, says when I shot that gun I did, and they know what they're talking about.

Let me give you Lewis Carroll as an example from history, who may or may not have interfered with his Alice—teachers discuss it behind closed doors. I'd say yes, from the sad look on her face in the photogravures Fishbite showed me once when we were on the trip. And I should know. *Post coitum omnis femina est triste,* not *sunt,* as we learned in Latin. And little girls, too.

But he wrote her such a great story. . . . Is the innocence of one girl child so important next to *Alice in Wonderland?* Does it matter if it wasn't quite soooo wonderful for her? A hundred years of beautifully bound editions? Can anyone honestly say that they would save the child and lose the book?

Anyway, some biographer says now that he was innocent, just a buddy of hers, you know, just an older friend who took pictures. Um-hmm, sure he was, sure. You think great literature comes out of nothing? Nothing can come out of nothing. Everything comes out of something.

7 As I say, Mr. Turkman was sweet, but in the end he did not get my mother more money. But she had something of a trust from her father and enough from Tex to buy a modest house on the East Side of Manhattan, too far up and unfashionably close to the East River.

She could have worked. After all, she was only thirty when we came up from Germaine. But in spite of her degree in decorating from Boggs Junior College in Marfa, Texas, she preferred to do nothing.

Actually, that's not true, she did do something–she drank exciting cocktails. Somewhere along the way, in some little antique store of the opulent kind she stopped at, she had found a book of cocktails from the 1930s. These she mixed in a thirties shaker and drank out of the appropriate art deco glasses from morning till night. I can still picture her, sitting in a round velvet armchair, in the slip dress, eyebrows plucked like chickens, sipping sidecars (tumbler) or gin slings (martini) and smiling mysteriously to herself.

Perhaps because of her métier, which means "profession" or "calling" in French (I will explain words where necessary–it is a privilege to go to private school and I do feel a sense of obligation), my mother was immensely fond of alcoholic jokery and collected things like sets of glögg cups in the shape of skulls, and lovely scotch glasses that had the names of different poisons engraved on them. There she'd be at eight A.M., drinking CYANIDE, or CURARE, or BELLADONNA and smiling mysteriously to herself.

And maybe this had always been, but I was six when I could finally see it. And I thought, when friends of hers said they didn't drink, that they didn't drink anything at all. And I was staggered. No milk? No juice? No sidecars?

She was always in a sweet mood, gentle, and liquid with sentiment. And she was always there, right there in the chair when I came home from school, right there even later, when we didn't get along so well and she wasn't in a sweet mood anymore because of Fishbite.

And if you drew a picture of my world from then, she would be in it like Gulliver. Huge and overwhelming to my Lilliputian doings. And yet, when you picture her in life, see her as tiny. Birdboned and slim, a round, dark-haired head on a lily-stalk neck, a slightly used face with smudged eyes and, of course, those crazy eyebrows. She was an old movie girl thrust into a world of cell phones and E-mail. She couldn't have figured out a baby monitor if you'd paid her.

She enrolled me in Hatpin, a private girls' school near the house, one known for the high-powered intellectuality of its girls, and there I went every day from nine to four, from the time I was six until I was twelve, dressed in the navy-blue uniform of scruffy privilege.

And at the end of every school day, I would tumble into the house and find her in the round chair, phonograph playing Latin music, sipping Cuba libres.

She was not always alone during this period. She did have her men friends, and many of them liked me.

There was Porter Cribb, son of a great fortune, and a fellow imbiber, who joined her in the chair when I was seven, and shared the cocktails. Together they planned vacations and then forgot to go on them. He wanted me to sit on his lap all the time, which I refused to do, chiefly because I did not like his aftershave. And though he took my rejections with good humor, he never really forgave me for it. He left us one day when, while visiting his mother, he got gout. He was forced to lie on his mother's couch for almost a month and found that he liked it at her house so much, he decided to move back in.

When I was eight, there was Lord Wally Krill, an immensely tall and reedy English peer who taught me the word "cadge," which in the king's English means "mooch." He was touring America when my mother ran into him at an antique store. She invited him home, and he stayed for eight months, until he went to study husbandry at a sheep farm in New Zealand. Though he seemed ancient, he was only nineteen. I liked him well enough and he seemed to like me, though he was always chasing me through the house, trying to spank me. I didn't understand him, really. I was, by then, exceptionally well behaved.

Then between eight and nine and a half, there was a pause. My mother took up with gay friends, and for a long time she didn't go out much in the evening. She did go out during the day, but primarily to fashion ateliers, that's French again for "studios," where she acquired clothes. "The better a woman dresses, the less she actually does, Lucky," she always said, "except for Mrs. Lustre."

My mother loved Mrs. Lustre. "She has such fun, darlin'," she would tell me after she'd observed the sprightly society monarch at an antique store or four-star café. "And that energy at ninety! I do envy her," she would sigh wistfully. "I do."

At night, in this period, my mother entertained. She gave dinner parties for groups of black-clad young men. They came and drank her cocktails and laughed loudly and then, by ten, went on to their all-night clubs and bars, leaving all women behind.

Then my mother, who often wore satin pajamas to these parties, collapsed in the round velvet chair and went to sleep, martini glass dangling from one hand, pink princess phone leaning precariously in her lap.

"I'm waiting for a phone call, darlin'," she would purr in her sleepy South Texan twang, "but I'm damned if I know from who."

Right before Fishbite moved in, my mother fell in love. The man claimed to be a gynecologist and a Muslim refugee from Serbia. His name, he told her, was Dr. Alba Cloaka, and she said she had the best sex with him of her whole life.

"Better than Tex?" I asked her once, referring, as I did rarely, to the long-lost father.

"Honey," she replied, "Tex couldn't find a G-spot if you gave him a map and lit it in neon."

I remember understanding only the tone of what she was saying. Yes, the tone said, a lot better than Tex, and I remember this shocked me because I was still under the impression then, as all girl-children are, that the one you marry and have children with is the best one of your life. Sally Jessy Raphael still believes it, which is why to this day I watch her program.

Dr. Alba treated my mother for a number of problems and was just about to open a practice in our basement apartment when the con squad called and informed us that he was a fraud. Not a gynecologist, not from Bosnia, not a Muslim. He was just a guy who preyed upon rich women and had bilked a number of them out of money.

My mother was crushed. He was married to two of the women even as my mother was planning the cocktail menu for the wedding. The con squad said that all the women he had snookered remembered him fondly, a fact that astounded me. Even my mother, forced as she was to give him up to the police, failed to denounce him. She just limped back to the round velvet chair and crawled into it. She didn't come out again until the day Fishbite turned up on our doorstep.

What I didn't tell her was that Alba once threatened to take out my spleen and sell it if I didn't tell my mother I liked him and wanted him for my dad. So I told her, because I knew that the way she was going, she would do what she wanted to anyway. My opinion no longer came into it. "Women Driven by Sex"–I've seen the show. They have no shame. They'll sell their children, not to mention their children's spleens. It's amazing how they cry about it after, sobbing on TV. Sometimes I think that grown-ups think that children are another species entirely, like little apes or something, as yet incapable of human sensitivity.

8 It was about this time that my mother decided to send me to camp. It was the beginning of summer, and on one of her rare forays to the liquor store, she caught me, sopping wet, running through the spray of an open fire hydrant with some poor Irish kids from the next block. She called my school and they recommended a sylvan setup in upstate New York dedicated to young girls and horses.

I liked it all right. The horses were docile. The cabins were snug and well screened. I was in Trigger. The only drawback was that one of the counselors was given to night visiting for what he called "summer snuggles." As the other girls in my cabin had no experience with this sort of behavior and were terribly scared, I captained our response and every night directed the others to push all the dressers right across the door and bar his way. It worked, and he left us alone and soon went on to Secretariat, where the girls were in their teens and yearning for him.

It amazed me when I learned that the other girls in my cabin were so unknowing. What makes one little girl honey to such wasps and another DDT, I must say, mystifies me. I only know I am that little dollop of peculiar sweetness and always have been. Is it something in my DNA? I wonder. Will they find it on the genome map, a flaglet hooked to some X chromosomes waving in pale pink? Or is it born of experience? Some of which I can't remember? Some of which I'm doomed to?

But it came home to me as I stared into the terror of these little friends that though I was lucky for my lack of fear, they were luckier still. For while I felt safety in my knowledge, it was the safety of one who has been in an accident and so no longer fears it and yet now fears it more than words and two small dressers across a door could ever express.

I came home after a month, unnerved by this realization, and having gotten breasts. I didn't like them. They made me very angry. They were just small puppy-nosed extrusions on the flat planes of my chest, innocuous enough, but I found them ominous and, even then, a harbinger of dismal things to come.

What they meant in the short term was, I had to keep my shirt on. "Keep your shirt on"—that phrase is telling, isn't it? As if to take your shirt off is the most raucous thing you could do? No more sun on my chest, ocean cooling my breastbone, air, gentle air on my upper torso. Now it was encased, entombed, it felt like, shut away forever into darkness. I would never be, I knew, like those women who pretend they are European, defiantly showing their breasts on the beach, never unaware, never unwatched. No. Shirtlessness was over now for me. And I came home, as my mother, if she were still alive, would testify, in a pretty bad mood.

9 The other day, in the library here at the facility, I came across an old article in a magazine. "Child Actress Gets Job!" was the headline. The story was about Miss Evie Naif, age thirteen, who, having been fired from a big musical a mere two weeks before it got to Broadway, has finally, finally, it's been months, found employment as spokesbabbler for a children's shampoo. It was, according to the text, between her and a cute orangutan, and advertisers went for the human touch. It still amazes me how her parents kept her name out of all our fuss. Their PR person must be awfully good or have some negatives in the safe. It's not that I regret it, really, but oh my ears and whiskers, it's her I should have shot.

10 I returned home from camp to find my mother a wreck. In my absence, she had taken to listening to shock jocks on the radio and to obsessively giving herself home pedicures. She had become depressed by the coarse and careless nature of what she had been hearing. Her feet were raw and red from the endless cutting and buffing they had endured. The cocktail book had been flung to one side. She was drinking brandy Alexanders. It was clear the thirties were out.

She had taken to wearing A-line shifts in lime greens and oranges, and wrap-around dark glasses. The round velvet deco chair had been replaced by a white plastic half-egg, inside of which were radio speakers that cackled at her as she climbed into it and curled up, womb-like, in the fetal position. A pair of worn white vinyl go-go boots sat forlornly by the front door. The whole scene reeked of the seventies. She had obviously had a breakdown.

"Mom," I said. I felt I had to comment. "You look like someone Elvis would have married."

"Do you mean that as a compliment, because I'm taking it as one," she replied cheerfully. "This egg I found in the back of a store in July and stole for a song. It has changed my life. I've decided to take in boarders."

She told me then that she was renting the downstairs apartment, once the future home of the Cloaka Clinic, to my father's ex-brother-in-law. Two husbands before the one who drove her into the lake and tried to claim the insurance, Tex's sister, Vanda, had been married to this Roger Fishbite, who was just about to grace our doorstep.

My mother knew, in her characteristic way, nothing at all about him save that his voice on the phone resembled a Texan Jimmy Stewart's. I remember at first warming to the thought of him. He was, after all, a connection, albeit severed, to the lost paternal figure of my dreams.

Then I turned against him. He was just another daddy on the lam, elusive and risky. I decided to have little to do with him.

But as luck would have it, my mother was in the bathroom when he rang the doorbell, and I was forced to answer it.

As I have already said, Dear Readers and Watchers of tabloid TV and press, he looked just like my father. I suppose I should have expected that, as my father's sister had married him. Warma Moneytree had a show about it once—

"Marrying Your Family's Doubles: The Freudian Truth." It was amazing. People just went right out and found spouses who looked exactly like members of their own family. It had something to do with comfort and possession, the experts said, and getting the relationship right, oh, and fear of the unknown, which, frankly, I don't have.

But Fishbite was the same type of big, blond, tall Texan, and when I opened the door and saw him, my heart tumbled around in my chest as if it had gone wild. And I was spell-bound. And then I searched for this dot above his ear, this dot I used to touch when I had my dad around, and it wasn't there. It wasn't him. And though I realized he wasn't my dad, at first I pretended that he was, and from that time on, no matter how I felt about him, I basically wanted to pet him.

11

I have a diary from that time which I offer to you now as evidence of the spell that I was under. It's a Little Mermaid Diary, from the Disney Store, and I bought it after I saw the movie, which I loved. I still get scared at the point where King Trident goes berserk because his daughter disobeys and wants to love a human man, I'm not sure why. That never happened to me. And I'm not a fish, of course, though it is a theme in this memoir, isn't it? Funny.

The diary begins the week Fishbite moved in, and I have rewritten it. It was babyish and silly and, in light of all that's happened, really strange for me to read. I'm sorry if it doesn't sound much like a child's diary. Perhaps, Readers and Watchers, I never really felt that much like a child.

MONDAY. Played in garden. Spied on Fishbite. He doesn't have garden privileges but he does have garden windows. Sitting at rolltop desk, <u>bare-chested, boxer shorts covered with weimaraners</u>!!! Very long legs, chest as wide as a stove top. I don't know what that is he types on, some sort of typewriter? But it doesn't plug in. Thought he saw me but I'm not sure. Anyway, I ran.

TUESDAY. Mom at Fishbite's. She took him towels and sheets and spent a lot of time touching his things. Then she perched herself on the rolltop and crossed her legs in front of him. I don't like the way she's behaving. I don't think he likes it either. He seems embarrassed and often turns his head away toward the window!!!

WEDNESDAY. Fishbite in shower. He left the door open, on purpose. I think I saw <u>IT.</u> Covered with fur!! Disgusting!!! I didn't like seeing it. I don't want to see it again. I don't know how grown-up girls do things, I really don't. Here's a piece of an essay I once wrote for school about it:

"Teenage girls get pregnant all the time, constantly. It's the biggest problem we have in the United States aside from child abuse. Every time I read any paper or listen to TV, they are talking about it. Now all of a sudden teenage girls are abusing and killing their babies before they even know them. I think that's really sad. I think you should get to know someone before you hit them. In a few months, I'll be a teenager. I dread it."

THURSDAY. Hung by the window today until Fishbite invited me in. It's a manual typewriter he's got there from the 1950s, of all things, a genuine antique. He doesn't use a computer, he says, because he's pure.

"Are you pure?" he asked me suddenly, with that fisheye revolving in its socket. "Stupid," I replied haughtily, and typed something on his piece of paper. That got him going. It was his precious story about love and sex, he said this last like I was supposed to jump like a bunny and run when I heard it. Instead I yawned. "So what?" I asked him, and his jaw dropped open. Then I laughed. He's pretty funny. I like him.

FRIDAY. I was just going in to see Fishbite when Mom knocked on the door and came in carrying a cocktail pitcher. "Lucky," she almost yelled when she saw me, "are you bothering Roger?" Which embarrassed me a lot. Of course I wasn't bothering him! He likes me and is very attracted to me! Roger—it's so weird to hear him called that— it makes him another person—bless his heart, piped up and said, "No. No. She's darlin'. So inquisitive." And he threw me a fisheye.

"Are *you* bothering Roger, Mom," I replied, embarrassing her back. And Fishbite laughed. "You know," I continued, "your apartment was going to be the Cloaka Clinic—"

"Go to your room, Lucky." Mom was seething now, but I didn't go upstairs. I took up my place in the garden and watched my mother produce two tumblers like a magician from under a cloth and pour BarcaLoungers—her concoctions—into carefully iced glasses.

I am proud to say that when they retired to the front bed-room, I didn't race to the front of the house to have a look. I'm not a voyeur—French for "Peeping Tom"—no matter what it seems like.

SATURDAY. Didn't hang by the window. Played in garden and refused to hear when Fishbite tapped on the window and tried to get my attention. Later, when the tapping stopped and I finally looked up, there was a picture of Michael Jackson's face taped to the glass with every other tooth blacked out.

I retaliated by making a Madonna scarecrow. I got one of Mom's bras and stuffed it all pointy and hung it round the neck of a broom. I cut a picture of her face off my CD and taped it above the bra and left it by his front door, which is down under our stairs, below ours.

In the afternoon, movies. *Hunchback of Notre Dame* by Disney. It kind of made me sick. When the Hunchback was trussed up like a turkey and covered with stab wounds and surrounded by a jeering crowd, I left the movie house. Later I dreamed that happened to me and I woke up screaming.

SUNDAY. Mom and I to church. My mother is a Baptist, of course, but she goes to St. James on Madison Avenue because it's Episcopalian and proper. I love the baby Jesus and I wanted to be a bride of Christ until I found out you have to work with the homeless. I feel sorry for them but I don't like them very much.

I never know what they are going to do and I don't under-stand why single grown-ups must live on the street. I know families do because I have seen them in documentaries of countries like India and Guatemala. They suffer together. But in New York it's all wild-eyed loners and I know about them from the news. It's the loners who fire on playgrounds and kill children. Always the loners. If you don't have friends, you'll probably end up killing children, that's one thing I've learned from TV. The only time I like homeless is when sometimes I've seen them from a taxi, all together with their carts and even laughing. This happens sometimes behind the Port Authority bus station, where I know from the news that young girls are often kidnapped by pimps. That's the only time the homeless don't make me feel nervous.

When I got home from church I went right to the garden. Fishbite was at the typewriter, wearing an elephant-trunk nose mask and pretending to read a paperback. It made me laugh really hard and I fell on the ground and cut my knee on a sharp piece of paving stone. I was bleeding and Fishbite opened the window and insisted on "kissing my boo-boo." "You're drinking my blood," I shrieked. "Vampire!" And I yanked my knee away from his lips. The way his lips felt on my skin made me shaky and out of breath. I'm beginning to understand something but I'm not sure what it is.

MONDAY. Must see Fishbite every day! I have to! I really like him. Mom likes him too and I'm really mad about it. I don't see why she has to like him too, even though I watched that Jenny Jones–"My Mother Stole My Boyfriend"–and taped it and watched it several times more.

It seems that some men like older women. They need mothering that they didn't get when they were small. I guess that's what happened to Fishbite. At dinner tomorrow–he's coming up to our house–I'm going to ask him.

TUESDAY. I didn't talk to Fishbite through the whole dinner. I saw Mom with him again and I'm not talking to her either. She told me they were dating and I wanted to bite her. I'd go back to playing with my friends in the neighborhood but there's too many homeless out there and someone could take me. Home is still the safest place for me, I think.

WEDNESDAY. Fishbite out in the garden–looking for ME, I could tell. He was pretending he was planting petunias but he kept looking around like a spy and I could see he wanted to be found.

I stood at the top of the garden stairs and stared down at him like I had X-ray vision, like I was the Cat Woman in *Batman*. I hissed and bared my claws.

He leaped back in mock fright–"mock," which means "faux," which is French for "fake"–fake fright and fell on the ground, then he leaped up. I ran down the stairs at top speed and head-butted him against the garden wall, which shocked him right out of breath. He grabbed me by the arms and turned me upside down and shook me until all my micro worlds fell out of my pockets. Then he made a rude noise on my thigh.

I struggled away and disappeared up the steps and into the house. I hate him but he is so fun, really fun.

THURSDAY. Good day with Mom. We went to buy school shoes on the West Side, which Mom says is a good place to shop but no place to live. I got saddle shoes because I saw pictures of her wearing them to school when she was my age. I think she's the most stylish person in the world. But who is she?

Of course, I wear a uniform to school so shoes are one of the few ways I have to show who I am. So I guess I'm a saddle-shoe type of a girl. I look like my mother and I do respect her taste. Which is probably why we both like Fishbite.

We came back to the East Side and bought underwear on Madison Avenue at Bunnies and Bratlets, my favorite store. There I ran into Eglantine Flout, who is back from Southampton and needs a playdate. I told her about Fishbite and she said she got kissed in the country by a boy near the old cannon at the end of Job's Lane. It was the only place, she said, she could shake the governess, who was stuck at the Ford dealership paying for new shocks on the car.

She says Hannibal Murphy, age twelve, just kissed her on the lips, told her he had a cyber pet and that it desperately needed some food, whereupon he ran off into the toy store. How did she like it? How did it feel? "Horrible!" I'm quoting.

FRIDAY. Eglantine came over and we sat in the garden for hours, talking about sex. We know what it is, contrary to what Fishbite thinks, because we see it all the time on TV and in movies and hear it on the radio and we would have to be deaf, dumb, and blind not to pick up on this part of the information age. Eglantine intends to remain a virgin until she is married. She will not have oral sex in high school like the newspaper said all the kids are doing. I don't know about oral sex. I know I don't like the sound of it.

Suddenly, in the middle of this private talk, Fishbite opened the window and asked me, "What about you? Do you intend to remain virginal until your marriage too?"

Eglantine and I both screamed. "Get away!" I shouted. "Get away!" And we both fell on the ground giggling so hard we couldn't stop.

In the afternoon, we put on my mother's makeup and tried to rent *Leaving Las Vegas* with Nicolas Cage, whom we both love. But we didn't make it. The woman wanted proof of age and Eglantine's credit card didn't work. We were reduced to watching bits of it on a rerun of the Siskel and Ebert movie-review show, which I tape. We can't imagine spending day after day doing nothing, even though we've seen our mothers do it. But we aspire to it anyway.

SATURDAY. I took flowers to Fishbite. Just rang the door and put them in his huge hand and kissed him demurely on the cheek. "That's for being you," I said in my best Veronica Lake. He was terribly moved and clasped me to his chest and hugged me close for a moment before his hand started stroking my spine up underneath my shirt. "Hey, that tickles," I told him. "Scratch my back." Which he did really well, all the way down to the top of my bum, which made me stretch like a cat and purr. He sat me on his lap, which was not all that comfortable for some reason, and let me type at the manual. It's very difficult and makes me wonder about old books and the effort that went into them physically.

We were having quite a good time when my mother staggered in with her key. "Lucky," she barked, "leave this poor man alone. Now, darlin', now." And she rousted me out of his lap. He didn't look all too happy about it and gave me a yearning glance. But he went to the front with her anyway. "Spineless Men—Can You Change Them?" The answer was no. Montel Williams Show #50, September of last year.

SUNDAY. St. James with my Mom. She no longer has a hangover when we go and everything is very different. She used to wear a scarf tied at the back of her neck and dark glasses and sit with her head bowed and nod quietly to the rector when we shook his hand as we left. Now she sits straight as a rod wearing a big-brimmed hat and listens to the sermon and makes me discuss it with her later. She only drinks her cocktails at special times of the day now and is sobering up for Fishbite. Sober, she's a totally different person and I'm not sure I like her.

She used to care about nothing, really, not in a bad way, but she was very relaxed. Now she cares about everything and it's all a big drama and we have lots of fights. Especially about him. I tell her she's jealous of me and Fishbite and that makes her really mad and she says I'm deluded and I get it from my father's side. His great-grandma took to a wing chair with a small American flag stuck in the upholstery and lived there for the last thirty years of her life. Maybe that's why Tex went to Pakistan, to escape some destiny.

Sometimes I wish Mom would just go away. That something big would happen and she would be gone. Boom! Oklahoma bombing on East 83rd Street. Lucky, we have bad news, dear. Your house has been blown up in a terrorist act. My house? And Mom? She's gone, dear.

MONDAY. I can't stand her. She said I couldn't play in the garden because I'm rude, which means I can't see Fishbite. He's dying about it and snuck up to my room to comfort me when she was out antiquing. She's buying 1950s Chinese kitsch now and little by little the house is being covered with it. I must say I love the lamps, wonderful slanty-eyed princesses with lantern shades in deep reds and yellows. The stuff is not PC and our place is a monument to colonialism.

Fishbite wanted to give me an acupressure massage to relieve my tension and I let him. He told me he studied in Texas with a famous lama who knew of pressure points no one had ever touched before. One of them was right inside my thigh up near my jeedge and it made me too nervous so I squirmed away and got him concentrated on my neck and he did an okay job. I asked to see his diploma and he said he lost it, which made me wonder if he really had one or had dropped out before he got it.

Sometimes he looks and acts really weird. I don't know what it is but it makes me nervous. Sometimes when I'm sitting on his lap at the manual, he moves all around and fidgets and it doesn't seem very grown-up. And he sighs weirdly and sweats all up. I don't like him very much then and I leave pretty quickly.

Eglantine says it isn't normal for a grown man to be interested in a preteen but what does she know about love? She was born premature, and according to a science program I saw, premature babies often have bonding problems, which leads to chaos in their dating life.

Also, of course, I had to point out that all of the shows had those really young boys who were dating grown-up women. Some of those women got married and seemed pretty happy, happier than our moms have been. There must be shows with really young girls dating grown-up men but I didn't see them. That, Eglantine says, is because it's against the law.

She's right, of course, I know that, but who made her the love police?

What is horrible is that Mom says she's never been happier and Fishbite is the One. I reminded her of all the times she's said that and she said she was drunk those times and couldn't accurately judge it.

She's taken to wearing cheongsams now or Chinese pajamas all the time. She got her hair cut Chinese style with bangs, blunt at the earlobe. She says it's to celebrate the twenty-first century, which she claims belongs to the Chinese, and then she spends all her time kowtowing to Fishbite. I think he wants a stronger, more feminist type like me but I'll have to watch him. Men can be perverse.

12 Dear Readers and Watchers of tabloid TV and press, the entries end there.

That was how it began. Who could have predicted from a beginning of such innocence that I would spend New Year's of the millennium in a facility for wayward youth?

Of course I know from going to St. James's that shooting another person is a sin, a grievous one for which I should pay. And I don't mean to sound like the Menendez boys or that girl from Long Island but—but—but . . . I do know how they felt.

Look at it this way: Would Alice have shot Lewis Carroll if she'd had a gun? Or the Lost Boys, James Barrie? Shot them down in Kensington Gardens? No cute statues in parks, only ignominy and notoriety? The question is, should and will children kill back? If I get my own show, which I might if my book does well, that's one of the topics I will definitely cover.

And whether I should go to heaven or hell is for you and God to decide. Under the circumstances, it's a difficult decision, and each case is different. For example, the people from Disney think they are going to heaven but after *Hunchback of Notre Dame,* God and I know they are going to hell.

13 Sometime at the end of August, I asked Fishbite to take me to a movie. He thought it was to be *Hercules,* the new Disney, or something else with a G rating. My mother was out antiquing, searching the city for bound-feet shoes, her latest passion. She had the tiny pairs of shoes in little glass boxes all over the house now, and every time she tried to explain to me who wore them, she decided I was too young.

I finally got Fishbite to tell me the truth about them while we were in a taxi going to the movie house. He said that mothers wrapped up their little girls' feet so tightly that they could not grow, so they remained as small as cat toys. When I asked him why mothers did this, he seemed to be at a loss. "To keep girls at home," he began. "To make them marriageable," he added, and then the real truth, "Because it was sexy."

"I think we'll do that to you," he then announced and grabbed his tie and began to tie up my feet in it.

I kicked like a little mule and he clutched his stomach and moaned that I'd been ruined for ancient Chinese maidenhood, with which I agreed.

"And why was it sexy?" I asked him straight out, since it was he who'd brought it up.

"Men liked the little feet"—he smiled wickedly—"like they like breasts today." He looked at my chest and I shot over toward the window. I stopped talking for the rest of the ride and didn't start again until we got out at the movie house. I told you having breasts made me angry and I meant it.

I had chosen this multiplex theater because I was intent on seeing an R-rated film, and frankly, Fishbite was my beard. The film was, of course, *Leaving Las Vegas,* which was being rerun, only that week, for a Phoenix House benefit. I stood in a shadow of the marquee, putting on lipstick, and directed Fishbite to buy the tickets.

He protested, of course, but only for a moment. He thought about it and seemed to like the idea, to like it a lot. He bought two tickets and then rushed into a tourist shop nearby and emerged with a hat. Now, he said, he was prepared and we entered the theater.

The usher left us alone. And Fishbite kindly bought popcorn and soda, which cost about twelve dollars in all and made me wonder how poor children get to go to the movies these days. I concluded that they just rented videos, which made me glad about technological advances.

As soon as Fishbite and I entered the theater, the lights went low. We sat way down front, right in the middle, where I could see perfectly. The previews that came on were for three Hollywood movies in which—guess what?—children were murdered.

For a week, I had ceased watching the news because I couldn't bear to hear about the Japanese boy who murdered children, too. Children killing children is the saddest thing there is, but you would only know this if you're a child too.

It has to do with the quality of our communication. That Japanese boy was so far in hell, the only thing left to do is bury him.

I started crying like I would if I had my own show and Fishbite put his arm around me. I don't know how I would do a show on the topic if I can't stand even hearing about it. But, obviously, that is something I must ask the experts. Oprah and Sally are the only ones who show their feelings. They often weep silently in compassion and caring. That's what I would do too.

I put my face in Fishbite's shoulder and refused to watch until the previews were over.

The opening of *Leaving Las Vegas* was pretty embarrassing. I hadn't realized that they allowed such pornographic footage in Hollywood movies. I couldn't look after a few minutes. What they showed on Siskel and Ebert was Nicolas Cage laughing and having fun, which he does for about two seconds, from what I saw.

Even Fishbite was shocked. But he was also acting pretty crazy. When Elisabeth Shue came on and started hugging the girl's hips, I think it was lesbianism, which they have lectured us about at school. We are not supposed to be judgmental or afraid of it but several of us are not quite sure what it is. I tried to bury my eyes in Fishbite's shoulder but he was fidgeting so much that it was really uncomfortable and I had to turn my head away from him and hide my eyes in the back of my chair.

"Can we go?" I asked a couple of times, because, though I enjoy a good R-rated movie when I can get in, I really felt this was way over my head, so to speak, but he didn't answer. He was sighing loudly and gasping and really upsetting me.

I took one peek at one point and saw a fuzzy shot of a girl sucking on Nicholas Cage's finger, which was obviously supposed to look like something else, and I stood up and walked out of the theater.

I was really very angry at Siskel and Ebert and when I got home, I wrote them a letter.

Dear Siskel and Ebert,
I went to see *Leaving Las Vegas* on your recommendation and was shocked by it. I can't believe the Oscars were involved in such porno. Nicolas Cage was much better in the opera movie with Cher and should have gotten an Oscar for that. Did you know that children can get into R-rated movies and be damaged for life by such things?
Yours,
Lucky Linderhof

I was also very angry at Fishbite for his crazy behavior. He rushed after me onto Broadway and tried to take my hand. I snapped it away.

"You are too weird. I don't like you," I told him and hailed a cab.

When he tried to get in with me, I told the driver I had no idea who he was, which made the driver get out of the cab and Fishbite run down the street like a wounded animal.

14

The house was empty when I returned. I went up to my room and ruminated on what I had just seen. ("Ruminated"–that's from Henry Fielding, an author I definitely revere. It's a very useful word meaning "think about a lot.") As much as I'd wanted to see *Leaving Las Vegas,* I was sorry that I'd seen it. There was something about it that tripped my nervousness and made me stutter.

When Fishbite came home, he came upstairs and tried to make it up with me. I kept the door locked and refused to speak with him, I'm not sure why. I just didn't want to.

I called Eglantine and told her about the movie. "Oh God," she cried. "Oh God, it was porno? How disappointing. Porno is so boring," she added, which she had obviously heard from adults.

"It wasn't boring, Eg," I went on. "That's the last thing it was. But Eg"–I hung on her waiting silence as if it was her warm little arm–"I don't know about this sex stuff. It's deeply disturbing."

When my mother came home, I went down to see her immediately. She was coming in the door with deliverymen following behind her carrying a beautiful teakwood bed which turned out to be an opium couch. Mandarins once smoked opium on it in the old days, my mother told me, before Chairman Mao killed all the dealers. Other deliverymen were coming later to take away the seventies egg.

"Mama, can I sit with you?" I asked her. She was lying on the opium couch looking uncomfortable. It did not offer the nestlike security of the seventies egg or the velvet deco armchair. The opium did that. You reclined on it, that was all.

My mother looked at me quizzically. "Sure darlin'," she replied, and gestured for me to approach. I climbed in next to her and hugged her skinny body to my chest.

We lay like that, silently, for a long, long time, I snuggling in her warmth, she crumpled like a discarded letter in my arms.

Like a calm sea, the gentle rocking motion of motherly comfort washed over my nervous form and brought me back safely to shore.

"Will you always be there?" I murmured in her ear.

"Always," she whispered. And then she sat upright. "However, Roger and I are going to Greece for a month and Mrs. Trout will be staying here with you."

15 I could not believe my ears. I was to be left behind to start school while my mother and Fishbite whiled away the glorious month of September in the land of Priapus's birth. Thanks so much. Fishbite, the lying weasel, had known all along that they were going. Where once my heart trembled for him, it was now as quiet as stone. I hated them both.

Fishbite was contrite. That night at dinner—he now ate with us every night—he tried to assure me that he did not wish to go and even conjured up psoriasis to prove it. My mother took him across the avenue to the office of Dr. Abdul Naif, father of the adorable Evie, child model and all-purpose charmer. Dr. Naif was the well-known dermatologist to the stars. Fishbite was forced to have ultraviolet-light treatments daily through August, which he described at dinner as him stark naked with goggles on in a special booth zapped at intervals with rays while out in the waiting room sat Liza Minnelli.

He deserved it. They were still going away together in September, albeit two weeks later than planned, and I had a big fight with my mother over it in which I informed her that I knew of her wish to get rid of me so she could ruin her skin to her heart's content on Mediterranean beaches, where they don't wear sunscreen and don't care about skin care.

Further, I said, Fishbite wanted to stay home with me, his true love, which really annoyed her, and she blurted out that they might marry and I better prepare myself for it, which floored me.

16 The day after our fight, I was pressed into accompanying my mother to Seventh Avenue showrooms to choose her wardrobe for the Peloponnesus. Designer after gushing designer thrust his or her wares before my diminutive matriarch, one of the world's greatest natural models, as one of them put it, one who had dined at our house on more than one occasion.

I sat demurely and silently as she tried on capri pants in silk shantungs, and floppy hats of Italian straw.

"I want Chinese," she muttered and the designers looked concerned. "But, sweetie, Chinese women don't bask. They don't cruise. They never have. You see what we mean?"

But she bought shirts with Chinese collars and wide-legged pants, and coolie hats, as they used to be called. She was dressed perfectly for Greece, the designers cooed happily. She looked like a Chinese peasant woman from the late nineteenth century.

While I watched her, I thought about Fishbite and the pros and cons of their possible marriage.

Pros: In just a few short years, Fishbite would be getting older. He would be passing out of the thirty-eight-ish age that is so desirable in the romantic male and into that most dreaded of male states, late middle age. I would tire of him. His hair would thin. His eyes would become myopic. His energy would flag. He would slowly prefer to read newspapers than to roughhouse. Or he would aggressively pursue sports that had passed him by, appearing in bicycle shorts at most inconceivable times of the day. His trim waist would develop into what is so unceremoniously called a rubber tire, or, worse, he would suddenly acquire a stomach so big and protruding he would closely resemble a pregnant woman. The hair on his chest and beard would whiten and go crinkly. And he would begin to worry about his death, a mental state that affects every man and is most unattractive to every women. Yes, he would become cranky, difficult, and demanding, requiring round-the-clock nursing care, and as he had no *amour toujours*–French for "true love"–I would have to oblige.

Cons: He only had a few years of fun left and they were being taken from me. By my mother, of all people. She didn't need him now, for heaven's sake. It always took several years for her to redecorate her life; she could have him later.

Pros: He was amusing to have around and it would be a lark to taunt him with other men later. Young, strapping lads with enormous Adam's apples and lots of promise would barely notice him as they came to squire me around the city. "Good evening, Mr. Fishbite, sir. Nice evening, isn't it?" The thought of it delighted me.

Cons: He would be a jealous pain about it. He was already a pain and he wasn't even family yet. And I didn't appreciate him two-timing me. It was different in the case of the daughter of the movie star–she stole her mother's boyfriend. That girl took the power. But now her mother doesn't have to have him in his dotage and she does. Poor girl, she chose to lose her family for a man. I blame her schooling.

Pros: I would be getting, dare I say it, a dad. A father, a patriarch, my own King Lear! Someone to buy ties and after-shave for on Father's Day. A person I could loudly claim "won't let me, sorry," or "gave it to me–isn't it beautiful?" A man I could safely love.

At my school, the daddies were in short supply. To be accurate, everywhere. I cannot think why someone would not wish to be a daddy, would not wish to be so loved. It is, I think, more evidence of the global neurosis of the waning century–don't you like that turn of phrase? It wasn't just the murder that secured this book contract, the proceeds of which I hope will send me to college when I get out.

Dad-eee. Dad. Pa-pa. Pater. Father. Fader. Man of my house. Strong arms that surround me, protect me. I like to believe that my real father is protecting bone-thin babies with no one else to love them. That he is doing good. I know he is. He did not abandon all the children in the world, as some other absent fathers have. He has some saving grace. But he is gone and I am faced with Fishbite as a surrogate.

Speaking of surrogates, in biology they showed the surrogate monkey film that shapes our culture. It said that baby monkeys preferred cloth mother monkeys to no mother monkeys at all. It said they had to have a seat of warmth, even mechanical, or they would sicken and die.

But I know from school that little girls get through it all the time. They have ennui and some depression. They often seem downcast when they are thinking, but that's all. They grow and learn and laugh and graduate with honors just like everyone else.

Cons: Daddies are scary. They can kill and hurt and shame. The tabloid asks if her daddy hurt the little beauty queen. I read it in the supermarket. I couldn't take my eyes off her. They found her dead in the subbasement of her house. I didn't sleep for weeks.

Eglantine and I are on that case, will be until it's solved. She was a little girl who loved her dress-up, one after our own hearts. She was one of us.

17 On the day of their departure for Greece, I kissed Fishbite. I had not really spoken to him for weeks, since the day before his ultraviolet-light treatments began, when my mother had first informed me of their trip. He was better, though not cured. His body was now host to 50 percent fewer red spots. Oh, the heartbreak!

Dr. Naif had prescribed six months of light, and upon his return, Fishbite was scheduled to continue. (That was, of course, where he encountered the unctuous Evie.) Meanwhile, he had bags of tar-based creams, which he had packed into a Louis Vuitton satchel even though, as my mother pointed out, Vuitton was so far out it was coming back in, but not yet.

My mother had trunks. Three steamer trunks, which Fishbite struggled under, finally lurching into the street, where a stretch limo was waiting. The chauffeur, a man of Arab origins, had not moved an inch.

He was leaning on the limo listening to a shock-jock radio program, feeling, quite clearly, that America was not only about money but also sex. The shock jock was discoursing loudly about some woman's breasts. I pretended to giggle and look away just as Fishbite heaved and tottered out under trunk number two. The chauffeur was leering at me as planned.

Fishbite was appalled. He grabbed my arm and yanked me up the stoop into the house, where he thrust me into a chair. Like a withered Atlas, he hove the third trunk onto his stooping shoulders and marched out the door.

My mother appeared from her bedroom. She was wearing a cloche hat with a veil, little leather gloves, and a neat Duchess of Windsor–type suit, and thick-heeled brown leather pumps. It was comforting to see her back in the thirties. For the duration of the voyage, the twenty-first century was on pause.

"Bye. Bye, darlin'," she chirped and kissed and hugged me. Her breath smelled like cinnamon from her lip gloss.

All trace of alcohol was gone. In a trice, she was out the door and into the limo.

When Fishbite ran back up the stairs and into the room to retrieve his one Vuitton horror, I leaped up and kissed him square on the mouth. I *was* going to miss him.

His arms curled around me. The warm smell of his sweat was strong and heavy. I closed my eyes and upturned my face as I had seen Ariel, the Little Mermaid, do with her prince. Dadee. Dad-ee. Dada. Dad. His lips touched mine and then I didn't want to anymore. I wiggled out of his grip and fled back down into the garden.

18 Mom and Fishy were gone and I was in the care of Chiong, whom my mother had hired through a friend at the Chinese consulate when Mrs. Trout fell sick. Chiong was a very nice Chinese woman of about thirty-six.

She had very thick black straight hair, cut in bangs, and falling to her waist, and she wore heavy black-rimmed glasses and early 1960s-style dresses with big skirts and petticoats, the summer style, evidently, in Beijing.

Her own son, age eight, was back in China. That first day she met us, she bounced smiling into the apartment and said, "Tell no one that I work for you."

"All right," my mother said.

"Excuse me, Mom, but why, Chiong?" I took over. I didn't want someone with me who was wanted for fraud or something on another continent. My mother was such a

Sinophile at the moment, she would have hired the Gang of Four to sit with me.

"My work leader would not like it," Chiong announced.

"This is a Communist problem?" I asked. I was actually quite excited about spending time with a real Communist. I read about them at school all the time. The Chinese and Cubans were the last of the breed.

"Yes." Chiong laughed.

She looked around and suddenly noticed the Chinese kitsch that filled our home. Peasants bearing pails of water on shoulder poles graced lamps and tables. Drapes illustrated Chinese pastoral scenes screened through the imagination of textile designers of the 1940s. Then there was, of course, the opium couch, now complete with opium pipes, lamps, and all the contraband equipment of the pre-Communist era.

"We won't tell," I said quickly.

"You smoke opium?" she asked my mother. She seemed upset.

My mother laughed.

"No, dear. I was born too late, sadly. I only drink. But I do love Chinese antiques, don't you?"

Chiong didn't really understand but she needed the job. Her husband was a diplomat but it was clear she wanted cash. She was hired to stay with me for the first three weeks in September, when my mother and Fishbite would be gone.

Chiong came into the room and watched me staring at the limo as it rolled away.

"You sad?" she asked.

"What a funny question," I answered. I hadn't a clue how to reply.

19

The weeks passed productively. I reentered school. Chiong went with me to purchase new uniforms, of which she approved because they erased class differences. And every day she walked me the two blocks to the school building, a companionship I had never enjoyed before, as my mother usually slept until noon and was virtually unwakable until that time.

Chiong insisted on accompanying me, I believe, because the week I went back to school a Chinese girl of my age was kidnapped and murdered in Chinatown. She was newly arrived from mainland China, as Chiong was, and the police thought it was a homeless man who got her. The girl just didn't know that as a child, she was in danger at all times here in America. Someone should have told her.

I saw a picture of her mother in the newspaper. The woman's face was a gasp of anguish. "A witness" had seen her child on the subway with a bearded Caucasian man. The girl was "very distressed," the witness told the police.

I wondered about that phrase "very distressed." I wondered that the moment was so memorable to the witness and yet the person had not mentioned it to the ticket taker in the booth, or to a transit cop. That's all the person had to do. But they obviously decided that the girl was a bad child, a reprimanded child, a child in trouble for good reason, not to be helped, not to be saved from a permanent time-out.

I tried to enlighten Chiong but she could not understand.

"They don't like us here," I told her. "If you watch and listen, you'll hear—they don't enjoy us children. And many of us are murdered every year."

"Like the Chinese girl?" Chiong looked horrified.

I had to reassure her.

"No, Chiong, it's really rare for a stranger to do it. By their own families and friends, mostly. By people they know and love."

"You have a one-child policy too?" Chiong was perplexed.

"No, Chiong," I said. "We have a terrible fear of the future."

20 While Fishbite and my mother were away, I hung out in Fishbite's rooms. On the wall in one corner were a dozen or so oil paintings of mules, which I now examined more carefully.

Fishbite had been born, he told me one day sitting at the manual, in Lubbock, Texas, the middle son of three, to an unsuccessful cattle rancher. His mother went crazy when he was two, but instead of institutionalizing her, they set her up in the barn with paints and an easel and a bed and there she became quite a successful artist, one who was widely collected by patrons and museums.

The focus of her painting was the mule in all its glory and, in all, by the time she died at age seventy of a rattlesnake bite, she had painted ten thousand mule pictures, each one more bizarre than the last. Her price was $500,000 in her waning years, and impeccably groomed New York dealers would trek through the mud to visit the barn and beg her for a one-woman show. Of course, she was too insane to travel anywhere, which they never quite understood, in spite of the fact that she was always nude when they came in. They just found her "the most perfect copy," they told Fishbite, who would peer in the barn door at his lost mother during their visits.

Over on the rolltop desk was a hideous stuffed Gila monster, a birthday gift from his father. His mother's art supported the ranch. His father, who had failed as a rancher, took to illegally smuggling rattlers and all manner of poisonous reptiles from Mexico into Texas to be made into purses, belts, and gewgaws or sold on the East Coast as pets. That was how Fishbite's mother was finally bitten. A box of tempera paints was switched for a box of rattlers, which was put in the barn. His mother failed to notice the difference and began to paint with the rattler's tail.

Fishbite's was a harsh and sad upbringing. He despised his two brothers, who went into the smuggling business with their father and were, as he put it, "as mean as snakes themselves." He had married Vanda, Tex's sister, to get away from Lubbock, not that Vanda was any picnic in the desert herself.

She smoked six packs of unfiltered cigarettes a day and was therefore surrounded by a perpetual smokescreen. She was, like Tex, extremely intelligent and prone to flight. It was not unusual, Fishbite said, for him to awaken and find her gone. Some weeks later, he would receive a postcard telling him the date of her arrival back home. In the five short years they were married, she traveled, for reasons he never could ascertain, to Amarillo, Isla Mujeres, Taiwan, New York City, and the Bay of Bengal. Then she would hop right back into their enormous ranch house like nothing had happened.

They got a divorce because Fishbite couldn't stand the mystery anymore. He wanted some answers and he just wasn't getting them. He was horrified to hear of her drowning some years later, but he wasn't surprised. "Men like to know where their women are, Lucky," he told me once. Under my thumb.

The left-hand drawer of Fishbite's rolltop desk was locked. I shook it but it refused to open. In the right-hand drawer lay a little handgun—I should say *the* handgun—which would later get me in so much trouble. He kept it against intruders, he told me. It had been a gift from Vanda, with whom he often drove to the Panhandle to shoot Coke bottles. I took it out and rubbed the smooth metal of it with my fingers. I liked the sound of Vanda, really. After all, she was my father's sister and could be expected to possess some of our family traits.

She had met Fishbite on a pier in Galveston, Texas, when she was twenty-eight. She was out at the end of it fishing for conch when she noticed him. He was twenty-five at the time and, according to him, very handsome. The minute he noticed her, a white-skinned blonde with red-painted toenails, he began having an asthma attack because he was so overwhelmed by desire.

As he lay gasping for breath on the wooden planks of the 1950s fishing pier, Vanda walked casually by and never looked down at him. Never tried to help him, didn't feel for him, couldn't have cared less. Given what he was used to at home, she was his type of woman all the way down the line. He grabbed her by the ankle and proposed right there. They were married that evening by a justice of the peace on the island.

"I knew your father a little," Fishbite said to me one day. "He was okay. You look like him and Vanda."

This was something I hadn't heard before. Did that mean I looked like Fishbite too? "What do you mean 'okay'?" I asked him.

"Friendly. Laughed a lot," he answered. "Your mother and he were a romantic-looking couple. They seemed to have fun. I was surprised when I heard he'd split. But you know, he was Vanda's brother."

"What fun?" I was drinking this in like my mother drank a new cocktail.

"Scavenger hunts. Croquet," he replied cryptically. "He was going to med school when I met him. In Galveston. Your mother and he witnessed our wedding."

"Did he . . ?" I was embarrassed to ask this but I did have to know.

"What?"

"Did you notice whether he . . . liked me?" I ran away over to the couch and buried my head in it. Fishbite followed me over and stroked my shoulder.

"Of course he did, Lucky," he said soothingly. "He loved you."

21 I was at home when Fishbite and my mother arrived back from Greece some three weeks later. My mother rushed up the stoop and hugged me. Fishbite rushed right after her and fell to his knees before me.

"We have something to tell you, Lucky," said my mother chirpily. "We're married!"

Fishbite looked at me with a hangdog expression. "Please forgive," he was mouthing but I turned my head away. I had to think about it awhile. As much as I knew it was bound to happen, I was not prepared for it, not sure I wanted a man in our part of the house, not sure I wanted to share my mother, my bathroom, my heart.

I kicked him hard in the knee. "I'm so sorry," I said as he yelped.

"We wanted to have you there, darlin', but it just seemed so easy to git it done," gurgled my mother. "There was this little white church on a rock and these incredible priests, very stern, and so much incense that Roger almost died. Right, honey?"

My mother was laughing and directing the limo driver, who was carrying the trunks up the stairs. It was clear that now that Fishbite was a husband he was no longer going to be much help.

Chiong took the steps two at a time and shouldered one of the trunks. It was amazing the amount of heavy work she had done while my mother was gone. Every piece of furniture had been moved and cleaned. She was wonderful. Fishbite was not shamed by her industriousness.

"It gave me such bad asthma I almost died," he said, getting up from his knees and staggering into the house. "I was prone on the floor of the church wheezing and gasping—"

"He almost couldn't say his vows but I got them out of him," my mother chortled.

"I'm still not right," said Fishbite, and he lay down on the opium couch. "Could we please get something more comfortable?" he whined to my mother. He was already starting, but she didn't seem to notice.

"Then I nearly drowned!" she announced, removing her gloves and sitting on the couch at its end.

"What?" This startled me and I felt my heart leap.

"Yes, we were swimmin' off this boat and I had given my swim fins to your new daddy here because he wanted to oil them or somethin', and I floated off and the current took me too far to swim back. I barely managed to swim to shore."

"Oh, Mommy," I cried and hugged her. Then I addressed her mistake. "Not my new daddy, thank you very much. I don't want a new daddy."

"All right, dear, whatever." She got up and busied herself directing Chiong to carry her trunks up to her room.

Midstairs, she called down, "We'll have to rearrange our sleepin' situation, Roger." And her voice trailed off as she followed Chiong into her dressing room.

"I missed you," Fishbite whispered urgently.

"Obviously," I replied sarcastically. "You're a traitor."

"No," he cried and endeavored to embrace me.

"Get lost," I hissed. "I know your kind—'Fickle and Frightening: The Out-of-Sight, Out-of-Mind Man.' I saw the program. It was Oprah and she was furious about it. Don't touch me, Daaaad." I said this last with utter contempt.

"But think of the things we'll do together," he stuttered, "the ballet lessons, the shopping, rowing on the lake. I take photos, you know, I'm quite skilled."

"The ballet lessons?"

"I'll take you to class and wait for you right outside. I intend to be a full-time father, hands-on." He wrung the hands in question unctuously. "You've missed so much. I'll try to make it up to you if I can."

"You will?" I asked. He was warming my heartstrings. I could feel them soften.

"Yes." He nodded passionately. "I like to do all the things little girls do."

For some reason, I believed him.

22 For the next few weeks, my mother busied herself with turning our house into the home of three rather than two. She moved a Chinese wedding bed, an enormous piece of furniture, into their room, and threw out the seventies hammock that she'd been sleeping in.

Fishbite moved up from the basement to sleep, although he still wrote downstairs and I still went out to the garden to harass him. We dined every night *à trois,* and Fishbite insisted, in his new paternal role, that I recite in detail the elite goings-on in the eighth grade at my school.

He especially liked to hear about what went on in the inner sancta, smoking in the bathrooms, or showering after gym, or anything to do with incipient sexuality.

At the time, Dear Readers and Watchers, I flattered myself that I and the minutiae of my doings inspired his undying new fatherly affection for me. Now, of course, I know he was just exercising his pathology, reveling in the toy touches of a girl-child's life. The older girls here at the facility assure me that every woman feels this way after a man betrays her. "Same trip in a different boat," they say knowingly. And I want and I don't want to believe them.

Fishbite resumed his treatments at Dr. Naif's, going across the avenue once a day for approximately half an hour to stand in the light box. His psoriasis, which had reached a peak after his near suffocation in Greece, was disappearing. And I, your poor obedient dupe-girl, attributed the sunniness of his mood to the absence of red spots from his fish-belly-white skin and not to his budding friendship with the child actress-model then known as Baby Evie.

It's true I did see them together, but I didn't think anything of it at the time. He was holding her hand, I thought, to help her cross the street. She was still so short, grown-ups felt they had to do this, even though she was almost eleven. She was flapping her great eyelashes at him and peeping out from under perfectly cut bangs, exquisitely dressed in the exorbitantly expensive clothes of Oililly, the Dutch children's designer. She carried her signature parasol. I didn't like her. I didn't want her on my street.

It was a long time later that I found out they were on their way to the park, to the boat basin, to go rowing, of all anachronistic things. Private-school girls were stabbing people to death in that park, and they were going rowing. "Let me see the daguerreotypes!" I would have demanded if I'd had the chance, but Fishbite wouldn't have gotten the reference.

23

It was after their return home that my mother and I began constantly fighting. I don't know what it was, really. I just had this overwhelming feeling that I wanted her to get away. I felt like she was crowding me all the time, even when she wasn't. I either felt claustrophobic around her or guilty and mean. I was pretty ratty.

My only solace was nighttime TV. I watched nighttime soap operas and police dramas and hospital shows, and, my favorite, the newsmagazine hours.

I now became the expert in my class at school on the murdered baby beauty queen. Before, I had only the supermarket tabloids to consult when the checker and my mother weren't looking. Now I knew everything—the layout of the house, the contents of the subbasement where it happened, and the details of the autopsy report, which, on the subject of molestation, was oddly confusing.

Many of the girls in my class, those who had gotten their periods, theorized that the mother had killed her. Hit her with the iron she used to freshen her costumes, Eglantine believed. Those of us who hadn't yet gotten our periods bet on a stranger. None of the girls accused her father, the billionaire with a second family. They all agreed that he didn't have the time. If he was home at all, even on Christmas night, he'd be on the cell phone and unavailable for murder. I trusted their judgment. If there was anything the girls in my class knew well, it was the habits of a billionaire father with a second family.

I always thought the ransom note was written by a child. It was the amount of money asked for, $118,000. Only a kid would think of that sum, a kid or a foreigner. I thought the younger brother did it. Can you imagine how much attention she got? He was the one with a real motive.

Every night, I locked myself in my room and watched TV. I took to eating TV dinners, which I made in the microwave and spirited to my room. My mother was furious at my lack of taste. Fishbite pleaded with me to come out, but even he no longer interested me. I began to fall in love with one of the doctors on one of the hospital shows. I lived for Thursday night at ten, when I could see the angst on his manly face. I paid no attention to the adults in my house until my mother fell off the roof.

It happened late on a very warm Friday night in October. My mother and Fishbite had evidently been drinking cocktails on the roof for quite some time. My mother had built a deck up there and was growing opium poppies and bamboo as part of her overall retro Chinese life theme.

Fishbite told me she was watering bamboo shoots when she stepped backwards a bit too far and fell four stories into the garden, revolving as she did so like a cat and so breaking her wrist.

My mother, who was quite drunk at the time, remembered nothing of what had led to her fall. For weeks after, she wandered about the roof trying to reconstruct the event.

"I never fall, Lucky," she told me, perplexed. "Never. Especially when I'm drunk."

I will never forget my mother lying motionless in the garden, her little body all at angles like a fallen puppet, her pretty face grey with reflected pain. She had lost one shoe.

Fishbite, for some reason, had remained on the roof—in a daze, he said—and I had gotten to the garden first. I glanced up at him, then rushed inside to call 911.

They took my mother to Lenox Hill Hospital, and Fishbite and I rode in the ambulance. She regained consciousness upon our arrival and refused to be examined without clothes. Instead she produced from her pocket a little porcelain figure of a Chinese lady such as was used by modest Chinese women with doctors in the nineteenth century.

"It hurts here," she said, pointing to the little figure's wrist. "I think it's broken."

And she was right.

24 After that, she no longer slept very well. Late at night, my mother would wander down to Fishbite's office and plan how to redecorate it. It became an obsession with her. At breakfast, she would propose changes, which he resisted mightily. I stood in the garden and watched as she pushed by him and opened the drawers of the desk, all but the one that was locked, which she stared at with keen focus. She bargained, negotiated, and fell to her knees, but in the end she could not budge him. He did not want the Ming emperor's writing tablet instead of the roll-top, not if his life depended on it.

25 Despite my having saved her life, or perhaps because of it, my mother no longer wanted me around. Though she had resumed her drinking—the happiness cure had not taken, as any twelve-stepper could have told her—she still waited for me as she used to, but she was no longer sweetly liquid. She was the whirl-wind wife now, even talking of having another baby. And I, I had seen something she wanted to hide. I was to be banished to boarding school.

She explained to me that she could not love more than one person at a time. She couldn't figure out the dynamics of it. And as she was the type of woman who could not live without a man, I would have to go away for a while, until she got the one love down. Then, she thought, she could add me to the mix and we'd live happily ever after.

She told me this one day as we sat on the Chinese wedding bed. Fishbite was at Dr. Naif's, whose name I cannot even write without my hatred of the cloying Evie rising in my gorge. She's doing a commercial now for a fast-burger joint, making it crystal clear, were there ever any doubt, that she has no morals.

Though I understood what my mother was saying, something happened to me when she said it. I began to sob, great heaving sobs, so deep inside my little chest that part of me lurched in surprise. I sank, along with my heart, onto the very mattress where eight hundred years of little-footed misses had seduced their big-footed men. How brave they were, those little girls who couldn't run. It was only their ghosts who shamed me then and forced me to sit up and live.

"Oh, Lucky, what is it?" My mother softened back into the girl she was before he came.

"Nothing," I answered, for I knew that it was futile. "I've got cramps."

26

I have not written much about Fishbite's oeuvre. That is because after it happened, when they searched his room, they didn't find more than two short stories and a quarter of a novel, entitled "So Long, Millennium," which seemed to be about a man in midlife crisis at the end of the century. He'd told me he had written much more, but that's the way of novelists.

The papers said his book might have sold had his life not been "snuffed out"–this is verbatim–before it had burned down to the wick. Poor, pathetic Fishbite. He struggled so with his work. Had he known how well he might have been received, would that have helped his pathology?

All I know is he had a fat roll of cheap paper which he would feed into his typewriter to type his novel, vowing never to tear off pages until the novel was done. Sometimes for fun I would unravel it and wind it all around his room. It amused me to see how exercised he got about it, really irked. He would run after me, threatening to spank me, and I would shriek at the top of my lungs, screaming for Chiong or my mother, slamming the door in his face. One time I hurt his nose, and I watched through the window as he clutched it, moaning. He deserved it, didn't he? The book of his that all America awaits is in my safe deposit box. It is, of course, his diary, a loathesome excrescence of a book that showed me no one can be trusted, no one, not ever, not at any time.

They say here at the facility that I am very disillusioned and they are right. But if I look around me at the state of other children, I know I'm lucky to be alive. No broken bones, no cigarette burns. Some mental scars, assuredly, but with some therapeutic assistance and a library of self-help books, I can lead a normal life. Lucky–that's my name. Don't wear it out.

27 Perhaps I've gotten off the subject. Fishbite. Miserable molester. Maniacal pervert. I was diverted to a criticism of his work. I am known here at the facility for my abilities in that field. I once published a criticism of Beatrix Potter in the facility newspaper, which, oddly enough, is highly intellectual. Did you know that Beatrix Potter wanted to be a botanist? She discovered a new genus of mushroom. But the Royal Botanical Society refused to let a woman join, or even give papers. So instead of painting mushrooms, she made up stories and illustrated them. Adults' loss, children's gain. One for us.

28

I was packing when Fishbite snuck into my room and sat down on my bed.

"It wasn't my idea," he said.

"I know," I replied. "I'm looking forward to it," I added. "It's co-ed, my first time at that. I'm simply longing to try sex."

"No!" he snapped on cue. "You're too young. Stay away from those fools. Save yourself for a man who knows what he's doing, who can teach you."

I gave him back his fisheye look. Fishbite blushed and said nothing.

"I read in *The New York Times* that there's a lot of oral sex done at these schools. Do you know anything about it?" I asked him.

"Do I know anythin' about oral sex?" he parroted back.

"Do you?" I now thought I might get some information out of him. My mother was sorely lacking in the sex-education department. She said she believed in knowing nothing, it made the finding-out more fun.

"Not much," he muttered, sounding for a change rather truthful.

They had at school, of course, taught us the usual biological details involving chickens and eggs, fetuses and spermatozoa. Eglantine and I giggled our way through the biological sciences, once becoming so hysterical that we both ended up in the headmistress's office and on a week-long detention.

"I read in *The New Yorker* that ninety percent of all women say they don't get enough foreplay. That's oral sex, isn't it?"

"I guess," he said and shook his head in annoyance.

"Women's liberation occurred as a result of there not being enough foreplay, wouldn't you agree?"

He looked as if he was about to shout something rude when my mother suddenly appeared.

"I'm not sure about this school," he barked at her, rising quickly from the bed.

"The old one or the new?" she asked.

"Both," he said fiercely and stomped off.

The telephone rang and it was a jubilant Eglantine. She had been distraught at my leaving and had worked on her parents to send her to boarding school as well. Her parents had finally agreed. They were so well connected, they simply phoned the place and presto, she was in. My mother was relieved.

"At least you'll be together," she said.

"What do you care?" I asked her. I was being provocative on purpose. I was really angry at her.

"I care," she snapped. "You know I care."

"I don't want to go. I want to stay here," I whined.

"I'm sorry, darlin'." She was as firm as I'd ever seen her.

"I hate you," I screamed as loud as I could, and she fled the room, holding her ears.

29 The Chutney School is situated on a series of green hills in the Pennsylvania countryside. For two hundred years it has been the chosen school of those wishing their children to lead our nation to prosperity and purity in race and religion; the Chutney motto is *Mundus sum. In ego, toto* (I am the world. In myself, everything).

I arrived in the main hall one evening in late October and immediately despised the place. The hall was an enormous three-storied structure with a huge fireplace at one end that threw little heat; there were several huge armchairs near it. The room was icy, austere, and academic.

A lot of other children were coming back after the weekend, and I watched as one by one, pale-skinned blond boys and girls with large sky-blue eyes entered and set down their obviously expensive luggage.

Not one of them seemed particularly happy, and all of them seemed resigned. They would give out no information about who they were until their parents left.

Fishbite and my mother hovered about, waiting to meet my housemother.

"I hate it here already," I hissed in their direction.

Fishbite hung his head. My mother rolled her eyes. At that instant, Eglantine shuffled through the great door, pushing her Bottega Veneta suitcases with her beautifully shod foot. She kicked her bags to the side and rushed over.

"Look," she whispered, inclining her head toward a long, lean boy about twelve. "One of the two campus dealers."

"How do you know?" I asked.

"I phoned around," she said. "I know him from Southampton. And over there"—she moved her eyes left—"the kids of the Serb war criminal, what's-his-name."

"Why do they come here?" I was intrigued.

"They have to go to school. I guess it's safer." She moved her eyes right.

"War criminals always have the nicest kids." I had always found this interesting. "That girl in the grade below us, the Cambodian?"

"Keema—adorable. The fathers take all their meanness out on the citizenry. At home they're fabulous," she said.

"I wish my dad was a war criminal"—Eglantine and I recited this together and laughed.

"Oh no," gasped Eglantine.

"What?" I whispered urgently. I was beginning to like the school a lot. If there's one thing I'd learned from moving in upper-crust society, you could not tell how crazy a person was from how they looked, especially well-bred children.

"Speaking of rape, Palmer Crunch—stay away from him. He rapes."

"He rapes?" I stared at the spindly lad with a blond crew-cut and half-closed eyes. Ugly red pimples dotted his face. He caught my eye and smiled back winningly.

"He's angry," said Eglantine. "He needs chemical peels for his skin and his mother won't take him. She's very stingy with her kids."

"Looks like he has that extra Y chromosome. How many girls has he raped, Eg?" I was getting scared now. I had forgotten that in every group of children, there are always a few psychopaths.

"What?" Fishbite was straining to overhear our conversation.

"That's the campus dealer," I told him, pointing the boy out.

"One of the two," corrected Eglantine.

Fishbite looked as if he was strangling.

"The class rapist." I pointed again.

"And the class seducer," pronounced Eglantine as one of the handsomest boys I had ever seen came through the great door.

He was about five feet eleven and already filled out, with wide, well-shaped shoulders, a tiny waist and hips, and curly blond hair. His blue eyes sparkled with laughter and desire. He wore a powder-blue turtleneck sweater, with tweed trousers, and a camel's-hair coat. On his feet he wore almond-shaped black lace-up shoes in perfect condition. His hands were big-boned but graceful. He had the neck of a soccer-playing swan.

"Oh my God," I blurted out on seeing him. "He's our age?"

"No, no," assured Eglantine. "Fourteen. A perfect fourteen."

My mother was off talking to an elderly woman dressed in a monochrome suit such as is mostly worn only by America's first ladies. In spite of her neatly coiffed blond hair with black velvet headband, she looked stern and suspicious. She examined my mother as if she were another species; her pink-rimmed eyes surveyed my mother's padded designer cheongsam with taut disapproval. I had warned my mother to wear the Windsor suit but she claimed the school was liberal. Nothing that costs twenty-four thousand a year is liberal, I told her, but she wouldn't accept it.

Fishbite was sitting in front of the warmthless fire, looking very glum. I walked over to him now and sat down next to him on the vast arm of the vaster armchair.

"Cheer up, Fishy," I whispered to him. "Now you and Mom will have all the privacy you need. And I, it looks like, will be having quite a time."

"Shut up," he grunted and refused to look at me.

"What's wrong?" I genuinely didn't get it.

He refused to answer.

"Darlin'." My mother strode over, followed by the stern woman who, as luck would have it, turned out to be my housemother. The woman's name was Cheeky Chippendent, the Cheeky a nickname left over from her days at the selfsame school I was about to attend. She was, evidently, living proof that one need not be the most well behaved of students to succeed there.

Though on the surface she seemed to have changed, in fact, Eglantine was quick to inform me, Cheeky was her old self, carrying on an affair with the school's anorexia-and-bulimia specialist, Dr. Manny Hart, who, it was well known, treated her shamelessly.

"Hello, Lucky," she said in a whispery voice. "Welcome to Chutney. And who's this?" She was referring to and feasting her eyes on the crestfallen Fishbite, whom I now introduced for the first time as "My stepfather, Roger Fishbite. Ms. Chippendent."

"Ms. Chippendent." Fishbite rose to his full height and addressed the woman in a stentorian voice. "I hope we can count on you to keep little Lucky from drugs, illness, and above all sex. She's an inno–"

"Dad!"

"Roger, darlin'!"

My mother and I stared at him, both horrified. Cheeky nodded gravely.

"Mr. Fishbite," she began in a serious tone. "At Chutney, we pride ourselves on keeping youth young and yet ahead of themselves intellectually. No drugs. No sex. And we even employ a medical specialist in the problems of pubescent females to keep those particular wolves at bay."

"What medical specialist?" asked Fishbite. He was suspicious of the whole setup and not, as he'd told me back in the city, without good reason. He had never gotten over, he said, the news story about the tennis pro who worked with private girls' schools and who was found to have a dungeon all prepared for a kidnap victim. Everyone trusted the man, it seemed, because he wrote his pupils cute notes with smile-faces dotting the i's.

Eglantine and I had met the man at our school but neither of us took tennis. The girls who did always talked about the man as a nut and a weirdo. They knew right away from meeting him that something was not right with a guy who drew smile-faces, same as I sensed about Fishbite's fisheye. You can't fool kids. They can smell weirdness a mile away. It's just that the weirder their own families are, the more weirdness they are willing to tolerate.

"Dr. Manny Hart." Cheeky smiled warmly as she said the man's name. "Columbia-Presbyterian. On the faculty. A genius in anorexia and bulimia." She hustled my mother and Fishbite away as she said the names of the conditions. "Manny says just by hearing of them, the girls can catch them. They are that impressionable. We'll keep her safe, Mr. Fishbite. Promise."

She crossed her heart and walked off.

"I don't like this place," muttered Fishbite, shaking his head.

"It's fine, Roger." My mother shushed him. "Oh, there's Chiong."

Chiong came in the great front door carrying my trunk.

"Where to?" she asked and Cheeky pointed up the huge winding staircase and led the way.

"Well, darlin'," my mother began, turning to me, and started to cry. "I'm sorry, Lucky. I'm going to miss you. Honey. But I've heard the food here is lovely for Thanksgiving."

"Thanks, Mom," I said glumly.

If I had only known that I would never see her again, I would have done things so differently. I would have pressed her tiny frame to mine and absorbed her like an ether. I would have rubbed my cheek on hers to try and cleave her face to mine. I would have looked at her so closely that I would have had a lifetime's memories for reflection. I would not have spoken differently—we didn't really talk. But I regret, oh, I regret. Can there be a worse thing to have to say?

"I'll be back Christmas vacation, Mom, if you don't mind," I said coldly and pecked her on the shoulder.

"See you very soon," whispered Fishbite.

"Yeah. Sure," I replied and rolled my eyes in exasperation. I didn't take him at his word. But how I wish I had.

30 I haven't spoken much of the facility, Dear Readers and Watchers. But it's a far cry from the Chutney School, as you can imagine. All manner of bizarre children are here, and it reminds me of what I've read of displaced children's camps after World War II. What was that book–*The Painted Bird*, by Kosinski, was it? He was an abused child too, I could tell by the look of him on the jacket flap.

Am I sad to be here? Yes, but no. I know that I must pay for what I did, under God, indivisible. Some kids here don't know that. They had nothing in their lives. It boggles the mind. It's their parents who should pay. You can't take a tiny human and hurt it and then expect it to give love. No matter what they say at Harvard research institutes, kids imprint like ducks.

Do they rape here? That's what you want to know, and why not? The press whets your appetite for that, you've got to satiate it. I understand. Not long ago, on the cover of our city's most prestigious newspaper, I read a story about the child sex industry in Thailand. It purported to be concerned and yet it opened with a man tweaking the nipple of a child prostitute, something factual and yet destined to sell papers. I felt, when I read it, as if that child was me. The point of the story was slim–now that Thailand's rich, nothing's changed in child exploitation. I'll say, and in New York as well.

And the answer is, they rape–some do–like anywhere. Even at Chutney, some did. Did they rape me? Not without my consent they didn't.

31

There were certain times of the day when the Chutney School was really quite beautiful. I especially liked the dusk of late winter afternoons when the dying sun coughed its last reddish rays onto the snow-covered playing fields.

I often sat on a window seat in that bookish place and read the works of Laurens van der Post, the great explorer. Someday, I thought, I might explore the great wide world outside—and I still might. I'll be in my early twenties when I get out. That's not too old for fun.

I didn't really miss my mother. Our fights had begun to unnerve me and I was glad of the separation. I pined a bit for Fishbite at first, but I was so intrigued by the Perfect Fourteen, as Eglantine and I dubbed the class seducer, and by the other characters at the school that I no longer thought about home much. Fishbite wrote me a couple of letters, which my lawyer later tried to use in my defense at the trial, but which were deemed inadmissable by a judge hostile to both femininity and youth.

November 20, 1996

My dear Lucky Lady,
How I miss you and your shocking garden hijinx. Nobody spies on me now at all and life is terminally boring. I'd like to take you to an R-rated movie again or possibly buy you some records whose lyrics are off-limits. Got anything in mind, sugar?

RF

I lived with Eglantine in a small room in a dormitory called Virginia Woolf, which was reserved for freshman and sophomores. The juniors and seniors lived in Sylvia Plath. The faculty, and especially the famous Dr. Manny Hart, lived in Emily Brontë, a fitting place, as Dr. Hart never stopped telling us, because Emily had lain down on the sofa and starved herself to death and was one of the early well-known anorexics.

"Karen Carpenter, the seventies pop singer, and Audrey Hepburn, the movie star, and dear Princess Diana were not the only ones," he was fond of muttering.

Dr. Hart often spoke to us after meals, inspirational lectures designed to keep us from vomiting for fun. He talked of "issues," "owning one's feelings," and other sorts of jargon that would never have been allowed back at our old school. Eglantine and I loved it and used it to make each other laugh.

"Oral sex is my issue," Eg would begin. We were now familiar with the term and used it freely.

"Own your oral sex," I would reply encouragingly.

"With the Perfect Fourteen?" she would ask seriously.

"Own his lap," I would answer and we both would scream.

To say that puberty had entered the picture would be a gross understatement. Puberty was my picture at this juncture. I ate and slept puberty. It controlled my moods, the health of my body, the look of my face. And all of a sudden, it gave me some hips.

This development was especially pleasing to the school custodian, a jovial and rather beastly man named Lorenzo

Morales. He immediately noticed my new waist and felt not only compelled to comment on it but to try to encircle it with his great pawlike hands.

I told the school counselor, a Catholic priest named Father Coughlin, about Morales but he didn't do anything about it. He just lit another unfiltered cigarette and asked to hear the whole story over again.

"Like this?" he asked, doing a reenactment by circling my waist with his leprechaunish hands. "Like this," he cried again, until I gave up and reported him to Dr. Hart.

"And did you feel anger, sweetheart?" Dr. Hart asked me.

"Yes, I did," I replied. "I was, after all, going for help, because one jerk wouldn't leave me alone and here was this second jerk doing the same thing."

"The details are not important." Dr. Hart closed his eyes tight and gritted his teeth. "Feel the hurt, Lucky. Own the hurt. It's your hurt. You have a right to it."

"Yeah! Can I go kick 'em? Right now? Right in the nuts?" I liked Dr. Hart. He had a great effect on my psyche.

"No, you can't. No." Dr. Hart sighed in resignation. I could see there was something about this process I was failing to comprehend. "You just own the hurt, that's all."

"But what's the point of that?" I asked. "What changes then? There's no eye for an eye?"

"No, Lucky, you don't get back." He looked tired.

"I want to. I want to." It didn't seem fair.

"No," said Dr. Hart, and the subject was closed.

32 It was on December 1st that Cheeky Chippendent came into my room and told me that Fishbite was downstairs in the great hall.

A chill shook me as I descended the staircase. Cheeky had looked unusually solemn, and, of course, where was my mother? Why would Fishbite be here without her? It was all too ominous to contemplate. My heart was thumping double time as I got to the bottom stair and saw him slumped in one of the huge armchairs, looking like a rumpled suit.

"Hello," I ventured. "What's happened?"

"Lucky. Lucky. You've put on weight," he said ungraciously and rose to hug me.

"Screw off!" I said, pushing him away. I had learned quite a lot of slang at Chutney, twenty-four-thousand dollars' worth of ripe street phrases.

"Lucky, watch your tongue please." He looked stern and upset.

"Where's my mom?" I asked, dreading the answer.

"Your mother is . . . well, she . . ."

My body temperature fell instantly. I was ice-cold and shivering. I stared him right in the eye.

"What?" I yelled.

"She's been in an accident," he said finally.

"She's still alive?" I clutched at the straw.

"Intensive care," he muttered, looking away as he said it.

"Thank God." I closed my eyes and said it again. "Was it the roof again? What happened?"

"She was shopping for bound-foot shoes when a taxi raced up onto the sidewalk out of control and went through the window of Boxer Rebellion Antiques on Madison Avenue. It was awful." He made a sob.

"Let's go see her now." I turned to run and get my coat.

"No!" He said this sharply and I shuddered as I turned back to look at him. "Her face was badly slashed. Her lung punctured. They said no visitors. She doesn't even want me to see her. She begged me to take you to a hotel in the Poconos until she recovers enough to have visitors."

"The Poconos?" This seemed so incongruous that I couldn't believe he made it up. "What hotel? What's the name of it?"

"Lake Innuendo."

33 I packed my things and bade farewell to Eglantine and the Chutney School. It was not a moment too soon. I had all but decided to lose my virginity with the Perfect Fourteen, and it seemed to me then in my terrifying innocence that Fishbite was removing me from the lion's mouth.

My mother, I surmised (unable to conceive of an infamy that would lie about her condition), would recover in good time. Once we were in the van, I tried again to find out exactly what was wrong with her, but Fishbite was vague. Under the guise of saving me from unnecessary fright and night terrors, he said he would not go into details. I couldn't call her in intensive care. I would simply have to wait until she was better.

The best thing for her, he went on, starting the engine, was for me to enjoy my trip with him. I cried silently, face turned to the window, wiping my tears away as they fell. I didn't have much choice.

34

⊚∵⊚∵⊚
∵⊚∵⊚∵

To commit his crime, he had bought himself one of those enormous bullet-shaped minivans that so many families have, with dark-tinted windows and a touring microphone, with which he pointed out historic sites of the Pennsylvania countryside.

"This is Puttersville Junior High School," he said in an announcer's voice, "where teacher Abby Nutterly fell in love with one of her sixth-grade students recently. She became pregnant by him and had the baby, asking for therapy rather than the jail term so many felt she richly deserved."

"Gross," I replied to this.

"But true," he said glumly. "She fell in love with him on sight when he was in her second-grade class."

"What a freak." I was shocked. "I saw a show about boys and older women on TV but those boys were in high school."

"You find it so horrible that two people could fall in love with years between them?" Fishbite said this mournfully.

"Yeah, he was eleven, younger than me. What did she talk about with him—puppy dog's tails?" I grimaced.

"Chutney has changed you, Lucky. I was afraid of this." Fishbite sighed.

"Why? What do you mean, Fishy?"

"We used to be close, I thought." He sighed again, wearily. "We had an understanding."

"That," I said, "was before you married Mom."

I looked around the minivan. "This is really spacious." I was impressed. "You could live in here, or at least have quite a seduction going on. They used to do that a lot in the sixties. People that headed communes like Charles Manson."

"Most people who headed communes weren't like Manson," Fishbite protested.

"Oh yes, that's right." Fishbite's relative age had suddenly dawned on me. "What did you do in the sixties, Dad?"

"In the sixties, I took my share of sugar cubes and bothered no one," he said defensively.

"Did you protest the war?" I had never considered his politics before. I myself was a Republican at the time.

"No," Fishbite muttered. "I was too busy."

"Doing what?" I probed.

"Having sex, if you must know."

I laughed as Fishbite blushed. We were driving now through the most elfin part of the Pennsylvania countryside. White, glistening snow lay on the hillocks, and the bare branches of the slender-armed trees were clothed in diaphanous sleeves of ice.

It was very cold and crisp outside our warm, snuggly ambulette, as I'd now begun calling it. It said twenty-three degrees Fahrenheit on the readout over the driver's seat. I soon pushed down the persistent anxiety about my mother's pain into my right foot, which proceeded to fall asleep off and on for the entirety of the motor trip.

In the plastic box behind the gearshift, where people usually keep tapes, he had his well-thumbed paperbacks. "What's this about?" I asked, picking one up.

He grabbed it out of my hand. "A guy named Humbert. Men's stuff. Not for you. No princesses."

"I almost had sex last week," I said, picking up the thread of our previous conversation.

Fishbite turned to me with an angry look. "But you didn't. Right?" He barked.

"No. I didn't. Just kidding, Dad." I felt sulky from his tone of voice. "Why? You jealous? Like King Lear?"

Fishbite glared at me.

"Are you?"

Fishbite said nothing.

"You are!" I fell about laughing. "Great. Well, it was the Perfect Fourteen, as Eg and I called him. He was so handsome, Fishy. I wanted to kiss him, really badly. I wanted to own him."

"Spare me," Fishbite hissed, and then looked really downcast.

"Aw, Fishy, you know I love you." I said this pretty spontaneously, but I meant it like father love, not boyfriend love. Maybe it was my mother's illness, or the fact that I'd grown up more during my time at Chutney, but I was warming to the idea of his being my dad. "Could you take me fishing?"

"You still have some feelings for an old man like me?" Fishbite looked at me from under heavy eyelids, wanting, no, begging for, compliments.

I leaned over and kissed him lovingly on the cheek, letting my lips stay for a while, then pulling them gently away.

"I adore you, Fishy, okay? Is this it? Wow!"

I was referring to the entrance to Lake Innuendo, an enormous heart-shaped gate which, when you drove your car through it, played "What I Did for Love" from the musical *A Chorus Line*, which I saw and loved, over and over again.

Fishbite drove the car along the heart-shaped road that traversed the grounds of what was clearly some sort of theme park. We passed the Boom Boom Rooms, the block of accommodations where guests stayed; the Play Room, where there were games to play; the Giftee Shopee, which had a sign in the window that said "Bubble bath sold here"; and a building called the Mickey Finn Lounge, named after the man who, Fishbite reminded me, invented the medicine that people put in drinks in Veronica Lake movies to knock people out so they could search their rooms.

"Why is the lounge named after Finn?" I asked Fishbite, perplexed.

"Uh . . ." He hesitated while turning along the heart-shaped curve toward the Take an Alias Office, as the sign said, where we had to register.

"Why?" I asked again.

"It's a bad joke," he said dismissively, although on his face was a hunted look.

"Are they going to knock us out and search our rooms?" I asked. This seemed an alarming possibility.

"No," he said definitively, and parked the car in a space in the heart-shaped parking lot.

"I love the way everything's heart-shaped," I told him as we entered the office.

"Good afternoon," a little but very fat man said to us. "Just married?"

Fishbite got angry.

"We're just passing through while my wife is in the hospital," he replied icily. "We need a room with twin beds, for me and my daughter."

"No twins here, sir. Only king-size. Round or heart-shaped," the man said, his eyes twinkling at Fishy.

"Round?" I'd never heard of such a wonderful thing. "I want round, Fishy, round."

"All right, dear, round," he said, and for some reason added, "She insists on calling me Fishy. Funny, little girls are."

The little fat man stared at Fishbite knowingly. "Every room has a heart-shaped bathtub–"

"A heart-shaped tub!" I was beside myself with this news.

"Bubble bath can be purchased at the Giftee Shopee. And other toys," he said pointedly.

"You have toys, too? What a great place. Thanks, Fishy. I love it here." I threw my arms around him and kissed him on the lips.

"Thank you, dear." He pushed me away rather roughly.

"There is one key only," the little fat man went on. "If you want to take part in any activities, you must do it together and turn in the key." His eyes twinkled again.

"Kind of an enforced togetherness," Fishbite muttered.

He was shoving me out the door but I wanted to hear all the rules of the place and was pushing against him.

"We need to know everything so we can have the best time," I said pushing him back.

"The Play Room is entered by going down a slide," the little fat man was saying.

"What?!" I was ecstatic. I addressed the clerk. "My dad really knows what young girls like, you know. He–"

But I never got to finish because Fishbite, who seemed to be in a terrible mood, bundled me into the minivan and sped along the heart-shaped highway to our room door.

I took the key and opened the door to what was truly Sleeping Beauty or somebody's palace. There was a big glass chandelier, the huge round bed, and one huge armchair to watch TV in together, and everything was in shades of pink.

"Look at all these movies about naked girls and cats," I called to Fishbite, who was out carrying things in from the car.

"What? Give me those," he said grumpily, and snatched them out of my hand.

"The *Sex Kitten* one is about cats having sex–is that the problem? Because I've seen cats have sex, on the street once. They screamed like banshees. Where do the naked girls come in? Is it kinky?"

Fishbite looked heavenward.

"Why is there carpet on the walls?" I asked him.

"I'm not sure," he said, and blushed.

"What's it for?" I really wanted to know when I saw how embarrassed he was. "What?"

"So people don't get hurt if they're dancing and bump into the walls," he replied after a moment.

"That's very smart." I thought it was. "I want to tell Mom about that. She might want to do that in our house."

I rushed into the bathroom now and beheld the heart-shaped tub. It was fabulous. A pink-tiled sunken heart with gold faucets, it was about six feet wide and three feet deep. I could swim in it. Next to it was a toilet-like object with faucets that I'd never seen before.

"What's that?" I asked Fishbite.

"A bidet," he replied matter-of-factly. "You wash your parts."

"Parts?" I was teasing him now. I knew what he meant.

"Lucky! Stop now!" he shouted and turned to go back out to the car.

"Can we take a bath now, Dad?" I was jumping up and down and skittering with glee. "Families bathe together in Japan."

"All right now, calm down. You're getting overwrought." He was shushing me and looking around like someone might hear. He went to the front door, opened it, and looked out nervously. I ran outside and took a deep breath of the crisp night air.

The sweet pink room I could see back through the open door contrasted beautifully with the blue-white snow on the grounds. The block of rooms looked a little like a ranch-style dormitory from the outside. You would never have guessed the treats that were stored within.

Suddenly one door at the end of the row of closed doors opened, and a group of men and women came out with cameras around their necks and carrying makeup boxes and film suitcases. Two brawny types wielded a huge white piece of cardboard with mylar on one side.

"Look, they're doing a photo shoot." I pointed them out to Fishbite, who visibly cringed.

"What's wrong?" I asked him.

"I need a rest. Privacy. After your mother's accident, you know," and he pulled me back inside and slammed the door.

35

Dear Readers and Watchers, I felt sorry for him in that moment. Sorry for what he'd gone through and angry at my mother, God rest her, for what she'd put him through. And though I've tried to forgive him for most of what he did and for what he drove me to, it's that anger at her that I can't forgive him for. Could you?

36

"I'm taking a bath right now. Can I, Fishy?" I was rushing around the bathroom, trying to find the tub stopper, which turned out to be a large pink rubber thing in a heart shape, edged with plastic lace. I placed it on the drain in the tub and ran the water.

"Can't we get a tub like this for New York? Mom would love it. Can we call her and tell her?" I hurried to the phone but Fishbite stopped me.

"No, dear," he said brusquely. "In a week or so. But yes, she would and we should. I thought we'd go have dinner. Visit the Finn Lounge?"

"You don't want to swim with me in the heart-shaped tub?" I mocked him from under my eyelashes. He seemed to shudder.

"I need my dinner first," he said flatly and strode toward the door.

I got my coat and caught up with him on the winding path to the Mickey Finn Lounge. He walked quickly for such a big man. He seemed to have the nervous energy of a small squirrel trapped inside him. On his good days, of which this was one, I thought he resembled that big blond French film star Gerard De Pudding or whatever. They both gave meaning to the phrase "absurdly handsome."

I took his hand and squeezed it. I was now so happy to be at Lake Innuendo instead of at Chutney, and with my own dad instead of alone, I could hardly contain myself.

"I'm sorry to make fun of you, Fishy. I'm just kidding," I told him and hugged him tight right there in the cold night air.

We entered the Mickey Finn Lounge and I couldn't believe my eyes. Right in the center of the room was a giant champagne glass filled with a cherry-colored liquid that swirled and sloshed around and almost sounded like the sea.

We sat down at a heart-shaped table and were given cocktail napkins that had lines in groups of five crossed off as if someone were counting the number of times something had happened. Fishbite refused to explain these strange markings beyond saying that whoever the designer of the decor was, she or he should be fined for taste violations.

"A Shirley Temple and a Jack Daniel's," he told the waitress, who was wearing a red uniform covered with white hearts.

"A Shirley Temple," I said disgustedly. "I've tried liquor, you know. I've had champagne three or four times at holidays and part of a beer at school. Can't I have a Mickey Finn?"

I pointed to the special drink, which was highlighted on the menu.

" 'Knocks 'em for a loop. Ankles up,' it says." I read the copy for him.

Fishbite seemed to hesitate but then he snapped primly, "No, you cannot."

It was a funny dinner menu: oysters, T-bone steak with rhino-horn sauce, and ginseng tea were all the fare offered. I ate my fill, drank my tea, and suddenly felt so sleepy I fell asleep at the table even without the Mickey Finn. I woke up a while later in Fishbite's arms, outside in the frigid night air, being carried to the room.

"I want my bath," I mumbled but Fishbite gently put me on the bed and began to undress me. When he got down to my undershirt and panties, I dragged myself off the bed, grabbed my nightie off the double chair, and stumbled into the bathroom and shut the door. I stared at the glorious bathtub through tumbling hair. I was very disappointed in myself. I had waited all evening to bathe.

"Where's Peco?" I asked sleepily when I came out, pointing with shaky hand at the suitcase. Fishbite rummaged through it and came up with the only surviving piece of my infant sleeping blanket, a washed-out beloved six-inch-square of cloth that up until then had kept me safe.

Clutching it, I fell instantly asleep.

Toward dawn, I was awakened by a snuggling Fishbite. I opened my eye, smiled at him, and went back to sleep. Then I was wide awake and so, it seemed, was he.

"Hi, Fishy," I said, and put my head on his shoulder. He felt warm and good and I was very happy. I was just about to say "I'm glad to have you for my dad" when I felt his fingers play across my nipple.

37 It happened in a moment–the explosion in my brain, the psychic shift from being there to being once removed. You know the phrase "beside myself"? I was, from then on in. Those little slaves in Thailand, they are too–ten times removed. So too the little boys in rectories throughout the Catholic dioceses–ten times removed. And of course the children here at the facility–so many times removed you cannot count them. And though we're living in a decade of no nuance, that's just theory. Here on the front lines, as they say in juvenile detention, there are infinite degrees of casualty.

38 Something had happened that was out of place, "wrong for the room," they say in comedy, and with that tiny gesture I was changed forever. It was as if some doors shut in my brain and others opened, and cynicism, once an unknown quantity, sloshed along with hormones in my blood. *He wasn't what he seemed.* How easy it is to write it and how hard to understand.

39 I froze. Like a rabbit that thinks if it doesn't move it won't be seen, I was motionless but tingling with fear. Fishbite continued on, blissfully unaware of possible trauma, seemingly convinced, Dear Readers and Watchers, that despite our differences in age, height, weight, and batting average, we were in the same ballpark.

"Did that feel good?" he asked, smiling conspiratorily, referring to the nipple thing. As yet, nothing else had transpired.

I was so shocked I couldn't think what to answer. I no longer had any idea who was talking to me. And the question was as incongrous as asking whether I liked the sound of the match lighting after he'd set off a round of Roman candles.

I had my eyes averted and I kept them that way. I said nothing. I did not move. "Can I show you something else?" he asked, his fingers tiptoeing down my chest toward my navel, refusing to take the hint.

"No!" I snapped angrily. "No."

"Oh please," he whined. "Please let me." This took me back. I hadn't expected him to plead.

"No," I replied tersely and sat up.

"Can I show you later?" he pleaded. "Can I?"

"Maybe," I replied, primarily to torture him. "Maybe not." And we got up and got dressed in silence.

40

It was a waste of a heart-shaped bathtub. I didn't feel like taking off my clothes again that morning lest it encourage further incidents, and then, in general, I just didn't feel good.

And as we left the room we ran right into the photo shoot, which was set up outside our door and featured, of all people, the heart-shaped Miss Evie Naif, shivering in the spring line from Oililly.

Fishbite nearly had heart failure and hid his face with the Lake Innuendo newspaper like a criminal passing by reporters on his way to be booked. He pretended to sneeze to cover his terror, but he needn't have bothered. Evie saw neither of us, so absorbed was she in complaining about the cold and ordering people around.

We had been on our way to eat in the family-style dining room. Everyone was to eat together, at heart-shaped tables, and we were meant, as it said on a sign near the door, "to discuss what went on the night before."

"I can hardly wait to get there and tell," I told Fishbite, but he had already decided to forgo it. Instead, we drove to a diner that was staffed by the oldest German lady in the world. She seemed to be blind, deaf, and almost lame, but she ran the place and cooked the food.

"I like it here," Fishbite said, beginning to relax. "It reminds me of Texas."

"I want to go back to Manhattan," I said.

Fishbite said nothing but he looked guilty.

"What's the matter?" I asked. "What have you done now?"

He sat silent.

"I want to see my mother," I said crankily. "I want to see her now. I want her!"

The old lady lurched over with our eggs. Somehow, she managed to get the plates onto the table without spilling, which astounded me, as she literally threw them rather than walk one step closer than she had to.

"*Gut?*" the old lady yelled from the counter.

"*Jawohl,*" shouted Fishbite back. He was eating, head down, intent, as if he had not supped for days.

"You know German?" I asked him. I couldn't eat. I didn't feel well.

"Sure. I got German ancestry," he replied. "Texas has a lot of Germans."

"Oh." I stared around the diner. It was actually just the front room of a dingy farmhouse with a Formica counter at one end, behind which was a kitchen, and at the other end, six tables and chairs of maple-syrup-colored plastic wood.

"Is this Amish country?" I asked Fishbite.

"Nowhere near it," he answered through slurps of coffee.

"I wish it was," I said, and suddenly I started to cry.

"What's wrong, Lucky?" said Fishbite, clearly irritated. He looked around at the old lady to see if she was interested in us. She wasn't. She had fallen asleep in her chair behind the counter. Fishbite was visibly relieved.

"I want my mommy," I sobbed, and put my head on the fake wood table. The odor of old grease and bad food made me cry more. "I want to call her. What hospital is it? Please tell me."

I looked up at Fishbite and he was grimacing like a trapped rat. Then he squeezed some tears out of their ducts with enormous effort and sighed deeply.

"She's dead, Lucky," he said. "She's gone."

I was so panic-stricken I went into a kind of palsy.

"Lucky?" He was truly alarmed now. He got up and came around to my seat and clasped my shaking shoulders.

Out of my throat came a wail so low and sad it woke the old lady.

"No, it's not true. Say it's not true."

Fishbite hurriedly got me up out of my chair and walked me out to the minivan. He went back inside the diner and paid the old lady, who was now staring at me through the window. Her beady red eyes registered nothing. Perhaps by her age they were no longer connected to her thoughts at all.

I had grieved once before in my short life, for my father, so I knew the waves and heaves to come, the mechanism of what engulfed me. But I have never known such pain.

Crumpled up in the front seat of the minivan, I screamed with eyes shut tight. Every picture in my mind was framed with anguish—Mom in the little Windsor suit, Mom in the round velvet deco chair, the sleeping Mom with cocktail in one hand, the feel of Mom in my arms on the opium couch, her little body, my Mom, my own . . . Now there was nothing. No one. Just me and somewhere out there Tex, the dying babies, and somewhere back in Texas, Tex's father, now the guest of the Ice Floe Apartments.

The shock of my sorrow and my aloneness, Dear Readers and Watchers, unhinged me. The girl Fishbite drove now screaming through the barren winter terrain back to Lake Innuendo was not the girl he left with, not by any means. Nor was, I must remind you, the girl he left with the same one he seized from Chutney. Outrage upon outrage upon outrage. "How Much Can the Human Brain Take?" I saw the show on Ricki Lake and the answer is, more than you'd ever think possible.

We drew up to the room door and parked and Fishbite leaped out and rushed around to my side. He bundled me up and carried me, his hand covering my screaming mouth, into the room and laid me gently on the huge round bed. He dimmed the lights low and ran the bath.

The sound of water cascading onto water soothed me, as it does the mentally afflicted, and I ceased sobbing and tried to catch my breath. I was curled in what they call the fetal position, the position you are in before you are born. And I lay unmoving and crushed while Fishbite removed my clothes.

"Look, Lucky," he said, using a name I felt I no longer could lay claim to. I looked dully and saw him pour bubble bath into the heart-shaped tub and switch on the whirlpool. Suddenly the bubbles were everywhere, filling the tub, spilling over, and reaching up to the mirrored ceiling. I laughed in spite of myself.

"In," he said. "In." And he placed me on the edge of the tub and slid me into it. And there I stayed, finally falling asleep, I guess. When I awoke, I had no idea how much later, I found myself in bed, unclothed, with the heavy thud of sad reality sitting on my heart and head.

Fishbite was in the huge chair next to me, pointing the remote at the TV, flipping soundlessly from channel to channel. I watched through blurred, wet eyes as snippets of children's culture passed by—Lamb Chop, Donald Duck, Elmo, Barney, and the Waltons nodded and expressed their grief. They were all so sweet to take the time. But it did no good. I was, as so many other little girls had been before me, inconsolable.

Fishbite stopped on one channel that was telling the story of the little beauty queen's murder. There she was in that beautiful costume with white feathers, diamond earrings sparkling by her perfect blond little face, promenading around the stage with arms open wide. She looked so different all dressed up than she did in the video with her family. In that video she seemed gawky and average and like a nice kid, not charismatic at all. Tears ran down my face. He flipped on the sound. Her mother was still alive, it said. It was she who was dead.

Fishbite flipped again, and on what seemed to be a child-abuse channel, the announcer told of newborns being kidnapped, newborns in garbage bins, a little boy beaten to death during toilet training, an eleven-year-old who had never been bathed, and children stabbing children in New Jersey.

Fishbite flipped right by the new Barbara Walters talk show and Rosie O'Donnell. A new breed of show was coming on now, apologetic about the old ones, making up for all the mayhem with good-heartedness and health. That was fine. I was all for it. But I knew that my show would be like the old ones, full of the chaos of childhood, the pain, the dirt, the joy.

"*Babytalk,* starring Lucky Lady Linderhof. And now your hostess, Lucky Lady!"

I say: "Thank you. Thank you very much and welcome to today's show, 'Controllable Molesters.'"

Fishbite noticed I was awake and smiled at me. He flipped off the TV and came and sat on the bed and took my hand.

"Are you okay, Lucky?" he asked softly.

I didn't answer. I wasn't okay, of course. I would never be okay. It was astounding how self-centered he was. Another person's pain was like a picture on the wall to him, an object you could take off and put in the closet if it got in your way.

I was waiting for the inevitable and now it was happening. He removed his clothes quickly and jumped in bed beside me. His body was warm and soft and in my dragged-out state I was glad of that.

He began to touch my breasts again, which tickled so much I sat up and violently pushed his hand away. So he moved it right down to my crotch.

"No," I barked at him. "No."

He looked up at me, angry, and began to push me down.

"Okay, okay," I said quickly. "You can give me oral sex."

He looked shocked.

"Don't you know how?" I asked him.

"Well, of course I . . ." he stammered.

"Then go ahead. I want to see what it's like." I lay back, rigid, and waited.

For a moment he didn't move. He had an odd look on his face as if presented with a dilemma he simply could not solve.

Then he did as I asked.

41

Dear Readers and Watchers, I must stop here lest I join the illustrious company of titillators and muddy my intent. I am not so interested in the pornography of the affair as in chronicling the sort of man who initiates it. And Fishbite was, here, hoist by his own petard, if you will. The oral engagement was, for me, a little shred of freedom within the prison walls, and after some deep embarrassment, I got used to it and in the end rather liked it. Fishbite, on the other hand, whose particular pathology was being led, seemed listless and exhausted by the whole thing.

"And will you do me?" he asked dully when it was over.

"No," I said with irritation, for the thought offended me. "Yucchy. Never. No, I will never touch you. Why would I want to?"

And with that important question hanging in the air, I fell into a deep sleep from which I did not awaken until late the next morning.

Part Two

1 It was after this event that Fishbite decided that we would take the Christmas season to slowly eke out our grief in the countryside before wending our way back to Manhattan. I say "our" grief because Fishbite had, at this point, convinced me of his own sadness at my mother's death. It was not, of course, until I read his diary that I discovered the extent of his calumny.

The very next day, for example, after our first experience with oral sex—I say "our" again because, amazingly enough, Dear Readers and Watchers, he confessed to me later that it was his first experience too—Fishbite vanished. He was gone the entire morning, and it wasn't until the day of the dreadful murder that I found out where he'd gone. It might have been this knowledge that drove me to pull the trigger, I am no longer sure. I have tried to forget the events of that terrible day, for they cannot be reversed and tend to haunt me.

At any rate, it was in the afternoon that Fishbite returned to the room. He looked oddly refreshed and recently showered, and he informed me we were going to take a car trip.

"Where?" I asked, only half interested.

I would have been happy to remain at Lake Innuendo. I had that day become involved in a pinball tournament down in the Play Room with some newlyweds hardly older than myself and I was winning. The purse was up to fifty dollars, with which I hoped to purchase the most advanced of cyber-pets. It was helping me forget.

"Anywhere," Fishbite replied. "It will be therapeutic."

"You'd have a hard time convincing the local child welfare officials of that," I said rudely, which shook him up a lot. "I want to go home."

"Okay, we'll go back to New York," he said all too quickly.

"To my house?" I asked, suspicious.

"Not yet," he replied curtly. "We'll spend our Christmas at airport hotels and motels throughout the tristate area."

◎∵◎∵◎

2

◎∵◎∵◎
∵◎∵◎∵

We set off in the minivan under cover of night. The shoot had wrapped up that morning but Fishbite was taking no chances. I had seen Miss Evie Naif stamping her Italian-shod foot and demanding ice cream many hours before. The advertising people had finally enticed her into her trailer only by promising a personal visit with Buckie Cheese, rat maître d' of the children's diner of the same name, on the way back to the city.

It was conceivable we could meet up with her entourage on the road, but unlikely.

"Avoid Buckie Cheese," I told Fishbite. "Evie's going there." I noticed that he smiled sweetly to himself.

After just an hour in the minivan, I was bored stiff. For a while I sang camp songs, then school songs, then Fishbite didn't want me to sing anymore.

"Does this car have airbags?" I asked him.

He nodded.

"I shouldn't be sitting in front then, you know."

He shot me a glance.

"You know why?"

He shook his head.

"Because I'm too small." I yelled this. "I could get suffocated! Get it?"

Fishbite looked surprised by my outburst. "What's the matter?" he asked conversationally.

"My mother's dead and I'm being kidnapped and molested! Is that enough?" I screamed at the top of my lungs, which made me feel a little better.

"You're not being kidnapped," he said calmly. "Have you ever read Kerouac?"

"Jack Kerouac?" I had read *On the Road* for summer reading the previous summer. "Yes. Why?"

"I'm beat, Lucky, beat. That's why. It's just a car trip, like *On the Road*."

"I'm not doing drugs with you, so forget it," I snapped.

"No drugs, just American airport the beautiful," he said, thinking he was speaking lyric poetry.

"When are we going to get there?" I asked, more because it seemed de rigueur (French for "necessary and proper") than for wanting to know. To his credit, he didn't bother answering.

I settled down then and began staring out at the incredible shiny metal sameness on either side of the highway. The business of cars was there, lit up and gleaming. New-car lots and used-car lots; auto detailers and auto mechanics; gas station after gas station, full serve or self-serve, shot by my eyes and repeated themselves until they blurred like one of those art photographs into a single strip of pinky-yellow light.

Occasionally, a fast-food joint nestled in between, awash in a vapor of diesel fuel, oil, and smile faces, the only place to eat for another twenty miles. But food here was only an afterthought. This was a patois of chrome and steel and black rubber, spoken in high, harsh light by the tongues of men. Mile after mile, it was BOB'S AUTO, TOM'S TIRES, WAYNE'S USED TRUCK. This was the last bastion of pure maleness in the land. It was a very rare woman who aspired to SUSIE'S GAS 'N' PEE.

The metallic aura of the landscape, its unemotionality, its grime-or-glisten simplicity, did not arouse my sadness. Perhaps this was why men liked this realm. There were no hysterics, only mechanics, to confound and perplex.

But why they liked the food was quite another matter. Over a thousand miles of highway Fishbite ate Happy Meals and silly meals, Whoppers and nuggets out of buckets and baskets, always with sauce. He liked opening the little packages and finding the strange treasure foods inside and feeling, as he so indecorously put it, "full" after he was done.

Lying on a plate without the little boxes and bags and cups, the Happy Meal would have looked decidedly less cheerful. But Fishbite never thought about that. Nor evidently did the other men, the truckers and techies and car salesmen that we saw in those places. And I did wonder what this said about the American male, whose stomach, my mother told me once, has always been the thruway to his heart.

We could have stopped to rest, but Fishbite wouldn't do it. He drank lots of coffee and ate his No Doz and was determined to drive straight through to the Newark Airport Hilton, which was situated in the middle of the Jersey wetlands.

3

It did not take me long to figure out that the reason he wished to stay in airport hotels and motels was that there was rarely anyone there. The Hilton in the wetlands, for example, seemed virtually deserted when we arrived.

We entered the air-controlled environment around eight o'clock one morning and ate breakfast in a vast, empty dining room overlooking the swampland. We watched as planes took off while we helped ourselves at a kingly buffet table of perfect-looking fruits, muffins, and iced juices. The food, like all the food Fishbite liked, had no taste at all. The coffee, which I insisted on drinking now that I had had my sexual initiation, was hot but flat. I found it difficult to accept that things could look so appetizing that weren't. But it was just another aspect of the end of my innocence.

In different hotels across the tristate area, we were taken by incredibly good-natured people up to rooms with enormous king-size beds done in navy, brown, or green. There was always a color TV, always a deskette, and, thanks to the tinted-glass in the windows, always a grey-colored view. The controlled air made me feel as if we were on a series of space stations. The only sounds in the halls were the opening and closing of elevator doors. One seldom heard a human voice, never the laugh of children. Fishbite felt, I could see it in his eyes, almost safe.

And he became the pain I had predicted. He was after me all the time for kisses and hugs and was always pleading for other kinds of favors than those that I had deemed okay. Yes, I was still the one leading the parade. How, you ask? How did I do it? Threats and intimidation, I thought.

Never forget, Dear Readers and Watchers, that the dance of the dirty old man with his little Significant Other is a dance choreographed by the devil. It is, quite simply, wrong. And this little one, like most others, hated doing wrong.

I had not yet reached the age when doing wrong excited me. I'd rather have gone back to school and gotten A's. I was beginning to do well at geometry and, frankly, I missed it.

So, though I only put up with the constant trysting, what I did really enjoy was threatening him. My fondest memories of this period are of sitting in empty dining rooms, declaring in the loudest of voices, "Where are we? New Jersey? Here the age of consent is sixteen years, exactly three years *older* than me." I didn't really know the age but he didn't know that.

"I don't need consent," Fishbite would reply, annoyed. "Nothing truly intimate has happened."

"Taking a minor across state lines for immoral purposes is an instant twenty years in maximum-security prison." I wasn't sure if this was correct but then neither was he. "Nothing intimate? It's called sodomy, mister."

"Lucky!" He would always become terrified when I uttered that term.

"Not to mention that if and when you get out, they publish your address and phone number in the local papers." I loved the way he snarled when I reminded him of this. "When did you become a sex offender, Fishy? Common sense tells me I am not the first."

I said this but of course I did not believe it. I flattered myself, as the girls at the facility tell me all little ones do, that he truly loved me. Even the prostitutes with pimp boyfriends imagined they were the only ones. None of us ever considered there might be another in the picture, in the blur behind our shoulders, not quite out of sight.

"Please, Lucky," he would whisper as soon as the incredibly happy waiter disappeared from the dining room, leaving us alone, "please can't we make love?"

"Officer!" I would shout as loud as I could, and he would cringe. "Lose my virginity to you? What are you, nuts? What's in it for me?"

Then he would list the presents and clothing and trips we would take if only I would give in.

"You know, Lucky," he would finally say, "someday you'll be grown-up and you'll have to give something in love."

"I can hardly wait for that day and for the boy I'm going to give to," I'd say, and with that I would smile angelically and eat my corn flakes.

It was, I remind you, the Christmas season. The hotels were decorated with all manner of plastic trees and cut-out Santas. Heaps of empty gift-wrapped boxes sat around as fitting decoration for the empty hotels. After some thought, I began to demand gifts for any favors Fishbite was to receive.

I demanded to spend my afternoons and often my evenings in the many malls around New Jersey and Long Island. I loved them.

The comfort I derived from these air-controlled shopping plazas made the loneliness of this period almost palatable. For one thing, I loved the music. Sweet, sugary versions of Christmas carols emanated from each store, sometimes overlapping and melding into one gooey strain of tinkling sleigh bells and trumpets.

I loved the trees—white trees with blue balls, green trees with red balls, silver trees with hot-pink balls, and on and on. Live Santas, fake Santas, and reindeer of every size festooned these underground cities. Every now and then a crèche appeared on the horizon, and like a homing pigeon, I flew to it. It reminded me of church with my mother, and I stood before the baby Jesus and wept.

Fishbite bought me dresses for kisses and CDs for hugs, and jewelry for oral sex. He promised Europe if I'd touch him, Asia if I'd sleep with him.

"For one of those rocket trips to space I might touch it once," I told him. "But that's about it."

"You are cruel, Lucky," he said sorrowfully. "And don't tell me again that you've been taught by masters."

But I had, Dear Readers and Watchers, and there I was, wandering through mall after mall, through deserted hotel after deserted hotel, mourning my mother, being mauled by an amorous nut. I watched planes leave for everywhere, never with me on them. And always we'd have dinners in those empty dining rooms à deux (just we two).

"Where are we—New York?" I'd shout. "Age of consent here is fifteen, still two years older than me. They'll get you on statutory rape, but they also have this 'depraved indifference to minors' charge here, which I like a lot. I mean, that says it, doesn't it, Fishy?" I'd scream. " 'Depraved indifference.' Doesn't that sum it up almost exactly? Lawyers are not usually known for their writing ability but 'depraved indifference' is brilliant, no?"

He usually kept silent, shushing me at the sight of the happy waiters and waitresses.

On Christmas Day, which was also my thirteenth birthday, he threw a party for me at the Sheraton Tarmac at Kennedy Airport.

We were staying in a blue room on the twentieth floor. The place was deserted except for two bellboys from the former Soviet Republic and one waiter who was studying to be an actor.

The waiter, whose name was Tommy Todd, sang "Happy Birthday" as the two bellboys carried out a green cake in the shape of a tree covered with red candy ball breakers, which I knew was a private dig. Then Todd launched into "What I Did for Love" from *A Chorus Line*, which Fishbite asked him to do specially and which, I have to admit, produced conflicting feelings in me.

"Can we go home soon?" I asked Fishbite that night after our usual argument in bed.

"Not until you give in," he snapped.

"Then I'll just leave and go home on the airport bus," I shouted. "I know how to do it."

Whereupon he informed me that I was trapped with him, that the house in Manhattan was sublet until the first of the year.

4 In that time of traveling, Fishbite emerged as a boring man. He did not read books. His conversation consisted entirely of sports scores and the doings of celebrities, recounted from gossip columns, which he perused with unnatural intensity. Once, I tried to engage him in a discussion about technology and the future, and within seconds he was talking about what playground equipment would be like when Michael Jackson's child was ready for college—a subject so arcane I hardly knew how to follow it.

He liked to watch videos or pay-TV movies, and he worked out obsessively in the gym, though the muscles he built up there were only temporary and vanished if he left off a few days, which was pretty hard not to find symbolic.

He wrote his diary every morning from ten to twelve, and sometimes he would attempt to write a story or part of his novel, an endeavor that always left him swearing loudly and in a foul mood.

He was terribly jealous. I couldn't speak to any male when he was nearby, and only to elderly females. I think some of the hoteliers were on to his game, for they often smirked when we checked in, perhaps alerted by the last hotelier on the route. Perhaps by the end we were bold print in some constantly circulating airport-hotel newsletter.

Under the strain of his wrongdoing, Fishy's asthma returned, as did his psoriasis, and he was not particularly attractive to behold. He was reddened and scaly, and he frequently stuck a white breather into his mouth, which he told me was all there was between him and the wheezing attacks that would necessitate his going to the hospital.

His life was so deeply dull that preying on little girls was just about all he had going for him. Or maybe it was the other way around. In any event, he was no Lewis Carroll.

At night, after he fell asleep, I would cry for my mother. Sometimes I thought my little bones would shatter with my grief. I didn't really want to escape. There was no one waiting for me anywhere. I fantasized that someday I would go to Pakistan and find Tex. I'd be older and I'd walk right into that hospital ward with all the dying babies and I'd say, "Excuse me, doctor, I'm your daughter. Lucky Linderhoff, remember me?" And you know what he'd say, after he stopped weeping? "Lucky. Thank God you've come."

I wouldn't tell my father about what happened with Fishbite. After all, my dad stood up for him at his wedding. No, I wouldn't mention the many betrayals. I'd just tell him about Mom and the accident and maybe a long time later, I might ask him why he left her. Why he didn't miss us like we missed him.

Yes, late at night, in these tomblike inns, I sobbed my babyhood away while Fishbite slept. I owned my sorrow, Dr. Manny Hart, if you're reading this. I clasped my sorrow to my breast so hard it broke the skin. And then next morning, I'd get up and eat another tasteless piece of fruit and I was on my way again.

5

Was I in love with Fishbite? Sometimes, when the light hit his shoulder blade a certain way, or he made a game of chasing me down one of the empty corridors, or at a mall when he was paying at the register, I could forget the iniquity and a wave of warmth would rush over me and I'd have to kiss him. I did like him, after all. I always liked him or none of this would have happened.

But was I in love with him? I remember Eglantine Flout once discoursed on whether children could be in love. Her three-year-old sister seemed to be in love with a ten-year-old boy who had swung her around at a party. "I want to eat him," the three-year-old said with an unmistakable gleam in her eye. But was she in love with him? Eglantine asked. When she couldn't see him, the three-year-old made him into an imaginary friend and saw him anyway. "The origin of obsession," Eglantine pronounced.

Warma Moneytree says young girls can't yet love in that way. Sally Jessy agrees. Ricki Lake disagrees. Jerry Springer wants to chew on it. Geraldo is outraged by the question. Montel Williams abstains. Barbara Walters is a definite no. And I think, well, if rage and love are the same thing, and in this part of the waning century it often seems as if they are, then certainly I was in love.

But that was apart from the sex, you see, which was in a box somewhere off by itself. I put it away when it was over. Didn't think about it. Didn't want to. Twice removed as it dragged on. Then three times. Enjoyed it, sure–better than not. Would I have preferred to have a Tamagoutchi? You bet your life.

6 The day after Christmas, we set off for the Ramada Tower on Grand Central Parkway opposite La Guardia Airport, our last destination before returning to our home.

We went in the afternoon just as the white winter light was darkening, the minivan bumping over the badly paved motorways, crisscrossing beneath crumbling overpasses, driving closer and closer to the city.

We arrived at the Tower around five o'clock, and Fishbite parked while I skipped into the warm brass and carpet soundproofing of yet another high-rise hotel.

But here, something was different. There seemed to be something going on involving children, and the lobby was filled with beautiful little girls from around three to eleven years old, chirping and milling about.

It was a convention of child model-actresses, evidently a yearly event sponsored by their union, the American Federation of Child Laborers, and this year it was being held in New York. The girls were just checking in. According to the hotel Arrivals board, the convention would begin the next morning with an opening breakfast hosted by none other than Buckie Cheese.

I looked around in dread, but I could not see Evie Naif. With any luck, I thought, she had contracted cholera from a street hot dog and was down for the count. Ear infection was a hope too, or pneumonia, or Coxsackie virus. Children got all kinds of illnesses at this time of the year, there was little to be done about it, and sometimes they succumbed. There was always a chance that Evie was no more.

I was so shocked to see so many people in one of these hotels—and especially children—that I hung back on the edge of the crowd instead of rushing up to register, as was my habit. That is why Fishbite did not see me when he bounced in the front door.

His mouth fell open and he stopped in his tracks and stared. His head swiveled from side to side surveying the lobby garden of tiny human rosebuds. Moppets of all colorings and shapes twirled before him—golden-haired, black-haired, blue-eyed, black-eyed, straight-locked, curly-locked, tall and lanky, short and round—and all with the most perfect of rose-hued pouty lips and little ivory-white teeth.

He began to have an asthma attack, clutching at his chest and wheezing helplessly and loudly. The little girls, well trained as they were to mind, lest they have to leave quickly, stopped as one and looked at him nervously. I walked calmly to his side and asked him, "Should we call an ambulance?"

He gestured no with his hands; then, still wheezing, he motioned to the crowd of moppets to come near. They elbowed me out of the way. As I watched, unbelieving, he lay down on the carpet, placed four or five little hands upon his brow and got others to massage his neck, and soon the wheezing stopped and there he was, like the Lion in *Wizard of Oz*, reclining happily in a field of blooming poppies.

He glanced over at me with a look that proclaimed, There's more where you came from, and I stuck my tongue out at him in reply.

"Fifteen to twenty. 'Depraved indifference,' " I called out to him, and he blushed beet-red.

"What do you mean, dear?" one of the mothers, oblivious to what was happening right before her eyes, asked me.

I pointed to Fishy. "Major child molester," I said matter-of-factly.

"Oh," she gasped. "Oh. Oh, you're joking," she said laughing.

I had forgotten. It was a convention not only of child workers but of their Simone Legrees.

As I checked us in with my mother's credit card, behind me I heard him saying, "I am a film producer, madam—how did you guess? Yes, from Disney. Was it the twill pants by Lauren and the many-pocketed anorak or the baseball cap and the tasseled moccasins that gave me away?"

I turned to see him surrounded now by moppets and their mothers. Around his neck he was wearing an eyepiece such as film directors wear on shoots, an object that I did not know he possessed and that I'd never seen him wear.

"What's our room number, Lucky?" he called over to me.

"Deep Six," I replied and walked angrily away toward the elevator.

"Excuse me, ladies, and little ladies," I heard him say. "I must follow my daughter there." And like a wolf stalking a sheep, he ran light-footed across the lobby to prey on the one who'd been separated from the flock.

7 I can only characterize the rest of our stay as rather revolting. Fishbite was, of course, in heaven. With fake Disney credentials, which he produced from his briefcase, he wangled passes to all the AFCL events, including the talent show, which he ended up judging because one of the judges got sick.

Some of it was fun. I got to have my hair dyed by Mr. Bunny, the most famous of children's haircutters. He put in auburn highlights and curled my hair in ringlets so I looked like Shirley Temple. He adored Fishbite and said, "Honey, you're so lucky to have that daddy. If I'd had that daddy, I'd be in banking today. Yes, I would. Three-piece suit, wing tips, the whole number."

It was the same thing with Patrick Dingo, the South African children's makeup artist. He showed Fishbite how to make me up.

"Look here, you sweet man," he began, "a little powder on the lashes makes them look fuller. See that little blonde over there, the four-year-old? It's two hours in the makeup chair every shoot. Her eyes are too close together but enormous, you see? Like a parrot. It takes forever to part those orbs. I work like a dog for these ones, you know."

And I did have several conversations with some of the girls.

One concerned the little beauty queen. Some ten-year-olds who'd done the beauty-pageant circuit were discussing her.

"It could have been any one of them," said Mary Jane McCusack, a black-haired, lavender-eyed beauty with the kindest smile I've ever seen. "They are all capable of it."

"Oh no," replied Barbara Schmidt, a white-blond, doe-eyed minigoddess from Georgia. "I never had anyone do anything weird."

"That's because your dad's a karate instructor," said Florrie Wong, an adorable Chinese princess with hair down to her knees. "And he comes with you."

"Of course he does. He's my agent," said Barbara.

"A lighting designer in Connecticut grabbed my behind and called it a peach cobbler. Isn't that dumb?" said Mary Jane.

"Mine's been called a plum pudding," laughed Florrie.

"Oh, that," said Barbara. "Oh, well then, I've had my breasts called apple tarts."

"What breasts?" Mary Jane and Florrie screamed simultaneously.

"Oh, I forgot, you haven't developed yet," said Barbara dismissively.

Mary Jane and Florrie were howling helplessly.

"More like raisin bread," Mary Jane gasped out. Florrie screamed laughing.

"Up yours," snapped Barbara and toddled off.

"Have you really had a lot of trouble from men?" I asked seriously.

The two girls sobered up and sighed.

"Oh, stuff and junk," said Florrie.

"They can't help it," said Mary Jane. "We look so beautiful, like little candy women or something. Look around you."

She was right. I looked around and they were scrumptious, positively edible.

"But isn't it different—admiring and murdering?" I asked.

They thought about this for a long time.

"Hop, skip, jump," said Florrie. "I don't trust 'em."

"They do a lot of things for us, though, because we're pretty," said Mary Jane.

"That's true," agreed Florrie. "A lot. Is that your dad?"

She was referring to Fishbite, who was wandering through the lobby offering piggyback rides.

When I tried to answer her, I felt sick. "Stepdad," I replied offhandedly.

"He seems fun," said Mary Jane. "I don't have a dad."

"Me neither," said Florrie. "Left at two."

"Left at three," echoed Mary Jane.

"Where's your mom?" asked Florrie.

I burst into tears.

"What's wrong?" asked Mary Jane and she and Florrie put their arms around my shoulders.

"Dead," I managed. "Last month."

"Oh, God," they said in unison. "Sorry."

I stood with them, sobbing, feeling the reassuring warmth and throb of their little bodies as they pressed me between them. For a moment they were sisters, family, people who had to care about my future whether they liked it or not, whether I did what they asked or not, people who had to care.

Then a voice on the loudspeaker system called their names and they had to go off.

"Bye, Lucky, sorry," said Florrie.

"Me too," said Mary Jane.

And they both disengaged themselves and ran toward the elevators.

"See you later," they called. But I didn't think I would. Fishbite was beckoning to me. He had a perpetual fisheye amongst these candy women, as they called themselves, and he was constantly on me.

Slowly I walked toward him, and when I got to him, I obediently took his hand. What was I to do? I had no one else to turn to.

8 As we pulled out of the driveway of the Ramada Tower, I thought I saw Evie Naif looking down on us from a fifth-floor window.

"Is that Evie Naif?" I asked Fishbite.

He didn't look up. "No. She wasn't here. I didn't see her," he replied.

I looked up again and she was gone. There was only a polyester curtain in that window, waving slightly from side to side.

9 Of course she was there, Dear Readers and Watchers, but not until the very end of our stay. She had gotten into some kind of scrape at Buckie Cheese's restaurant and had been barred from the conference breakfast where he would perform. She had in her bratty way mistreated Buckie and been evicted from his place. Unceremoniously, her lawyer was quoted in a magazine as saying.

Buckie's people were adamant. He would not open the conference if she was there. She had been horrible to the mouse, pulling and pushing him and ultimately ripping his costume and kicking him so hard as to cause bruises to the gentle soul hiding inside. There were rumors about her of substance abuse and even of affairs with old men, but I never put two and two together. I always figured that one crime for Fishbite was enough. I had forgotten about how much more sense it makes to be hanged for a sheep than a lamb.

10 It was dusk as we left, a cold, clear blue dusk with shiny yellow stars. Fishbite drove along the parkway, then took the exit to the expressway; almost instantly, the skyline of New York City was stretched out before us. My first feeling when I saw it was relief that soon I would be home, at my house, in my room, with my toys.

All the time I was gone, I kept picturing my plastic beauty salon that I've had since I was three and still have here at the facility. It sits in a corner of the cell here, all pink and mauve molded plastic–an oval mirror and a little desk before a chair that swivels. I have always sat there and thought about things. I could hardly wait to see it again.

But as we drove down toward the entrance to the Midtown Tunnel, I began to shake. Just a little at first, then more and more, until, as we entered the tunnel, my teeth were chattering and my body was jiggling as if I had Saint Vitus' dance.

Fishbite glanced over and did a double take.

"What's wrong?" he asked, concerned.

"I don't know," I replied, hugging myself, trying to calm myself down. I could hardly talk. My chattering teeth and burbling lips made me sound drunk.

"Chiong will be there waiting," he said, reaching over with one hand and patting my shoulder.

"Chiong?" I hadn't thought of her in so long, it took me a minute to recognize whom he was talking about. "Chiong," I said again.

And floods of memories inundated my mind, all of them containing my mother. Grief rushed through me, pouring out my eyes and my mouth in wet sobs and wails.

"Oh, sugar," said Fishbite sweetly. "It's going to be okay. You'll go back to school, see your friends. Chiong will be there too. It will almost be like old times."

I was melting on the minivan seat like a dropped scoop of ice cream. I felt myself dissolving, spreading out toward the edges of my physical frame, diluting dangerously, definitely in danger of molecular meltdown.

"Sugar? Lucky?"

It could have gone either way. Fishbite was staring at me, horrified. I could have just let go and gone. And it would have been over in some ways, another kind of life entirely, with few responsibilities.

But I didn't want to end up crazy and homeless. So I sucked myself up inside myself in one big breath and went calm. As I recovered my composure and set about surviving, Fishbite said, "I love you, little girl."

I snapped my eyes to him. He looked sincere. I think he did love me, Dear Readers and Watchers, in his crazy way. At the very least he was obsessed with me. I was his first thought when he arose in the morning, tapping the sheet next to him and murmuring "Lucky? Sugar?" And before he lay down to sleep, he always kissed my right clavicle. I'm sure he really did care.

As we sat in the tunnel to New York City, I still believed he would take care of me through thick and thin, which is short for "through thicket and thin wood"—it's from Middle English and indicates that in those days some people left the forest when the woods got thicker, probably because of brigands.

Of course the question the girls ask at the facility—and many of them are extremely cynical, as you might imagine— is whether he would have cared for me if I'd denied him favors. They say no. I say I don't know the answer to that and I never ever will.

We were stuck in the tunnel for an hour. It was Sunday evening and the traffic was terrible. After a pretty long silence, Fishbite suddenly said, "You know you can't tell, Lucky. You know that?"

"Tell what?" Right then I truly didn't know what he meant.

"About us," he whispered.

"Why whisper? It's only us together in the car." I was angered by this but I didn't know why.

"You never know," he said looking around at the other cars.

"You think they have listening devices?" I asked him.

"I'll go to prison if you tell anyone." He was very serious now. All fun was over. "Did you tell Eglantine?"

"No, I didn't." I told him the truth. "But she was there. She knows you're weird."

"You didn't tell her at Chutney?" His voice was so grave I hardly recognized it.

"No, sir." That seemed the proper way to answer that voice.

"Because if they take me away, Lucky . . ."

I began to space out at that point. I was afraid of what was coming. I stopped hearing him and focused all my senses on the long white tunnel around us—the dirt-streaked tiles, the grimy air, the cars around us purring and squeaking.

"Lucky!"

I looked at him. I was very scared.

"You'll go to foster care. Like in the newspapers. With some strange family who believe in God knows what. You won't know if you can trust them or if they'll hurt you. No private school, darlin', you can kiss that good-bye."

"Most children are murdered by people they know." I whispered this to myself. It was meant to be calming but it wasn't.

"What?"

"Nothing," I murmured.

"I'm the only one you have left," he said matter-of-factly. "Your grandfather is senile. Your father is on the other side of the world and—forgive me for this but I must say it so you understand—he doesn't care what happens to you. I'm it, sugar. So if you tell, the plain fact is you'll lose everything."

"I won't tell," I said softly. I felt exhausted. I leaned back against the seat and closed my eyes. Tears rolled down my face and slipped salty into my mouth. Within seconds, I willed myself to sleep.

11 I was beginning to feel like I was going to explode. At different times of the day or night a huge rage would well up in me and I would have to beat something inanimate until it was, theoretically, lifeless. Sometimes I would just yell at someone until I couldn't yell anymore.

It was at Kennedy Airport's Sheraton Flight Path that I first had the problem. I was in the room alone for a change. I lay on the bed silent, staring at the ceiling for a while, and then suddenly I started pounding the pillow and screaming, and I pounded and screamed for so long that finally the phone rang. It was the manager; I forced a laugh and claimed I was doing primal scream therapy, which, I suppose, in a way, was true.

It happened again at the Ramada Tower. A little beauty queen dressed exactly like Marlene Dietrich in *The Blue Angel* almost closed the elevator door on me. The little blond dolly in satin top hat and tails turned out actually to be German and tried to apologize in a combination of German and English.

"Excuse me, mein friend," she began nicely, but I cut her off viciously.

"You little weasel," I hissed. "You almost killed me. Now I'm going to kill you." And I grabbed her wrist and twisted it as hard as I could.

"Mama!" she screamed at the top of her lungs, and I let her go and escaped quickly down the corridor.

Later when I ran into her in the lobby and she pointed me out to her mother, I smiled my angel smile and pretended to know nothing.

She glared at me across the lobby of tousled heads as if to say, "I know you. And you know I do."

I wasn't happy about this development in myself. I couldn't understand it. Out of me would leap this rabid ferret girl, leaving the rest of me standing there, ashamed and afraid. When the ferret girl leaped back in, I would collapse and weep uncontrollably. I would have asked someone about it, were there someone to ask, but since there wasn't, I became confused. Why didn't I ask Fishbite? you wonder–

my lover, my brother, my dad. Because he was doing wrong, that's why. And everything to do with him was suspect.

Isn't it odd, Dear Readers and Watchers, how it works? How intimacy is so often born of malice? People cheat on their lovers with new lovers and the new lovers trust that they'll never cheat on them. I wasn't one of those. I never trusted Fishbite. Not for a moment. Not after the nipple thing. No way.

12

I awoke as Fishbite parked the minivan and turned off the motor.

"We're home!" he said cheerily, and I opened my eyes and stared out the window.

There was the house, the little, skinny brownstone painted Beijing red with dead poppies drooping from the window boxes. I hallucinated my mother opening the door, running down the stairs, and folding me in her arms. Then I sat deadened in the seat, unable to get out of the minivan.

Just then the house door did open and Chiong looked out.

"You back," she called in her heavy Chinese accent, more of a statement than a question. She was wearing a white sweater set and a full skirt covered all over with a giant mushroom print. She wore an *Alice in Wonderland* velvet headband in her long black hair and, of course, her big black-rimmed eyeglasses.

She seemed younger than I remembered, possibly because her outfit, purchased in Beijing department stores, was so stylish. The only odd touch was her Chinese running shoes, which she wore with stockings. She hurried down the stairs, opened the minivan door, and helped me out.

"How you?" she asked, putting her arm around my shoulder and gently pushing me up the stairs. "You have nice Christmas?"

"No," I replied simply and Chiong nodded to herself.

"I keep everything same for you. Very important until you say good-bye to mother." She led me into the living room and sat me down in front of the ancient Chinese brazier that my mother had wanted us to use instead of a fireplace. Chiong struck a match and lit the coals.

I gazed around the room at my former life. The opium couch was still there with its golden brocade cushions. The enormous red Chinese prince and princess lamps with their pagoda shades still flanked it. The yellow curtains with their pastoral scenes of Chinese eighteenth-century life. And, still in the corner, the cabinet of little shoes for bound feet.

I walked over to it now and noticed that some of them were stained with blood.

"Yes," said Chiong, following my glance, "she bought those that day."

"Did you see anything?" I asked. In my life I was always searching for ragged shreds of information to get me through. Tiny details that others might discard had formed the memories I held dear and shaped my understanding.

"I went to the store just after your mother was taken," she said, holding my arm and leading me back to the brazier.

"There was glass and little shoes all over street. She just bought a new bunch, you know." She slipped into the kitchen for a moment and returned with a fragrant tea. "In ancient times," she said, "women gave the little shoes to make friendship. I have these for you."

She handed me a little shopping bag, inside of which was a lovely pair of tiny boots. They were no more than four inches long and clearly had been heavily used.

"These worn by working woman," said Chiong, pointing to the used leather soles. "In early this century. And on side"–she indicated the embroidered pattern–"is bamboo for endurance and longevity."

I held the little boots in the palm of my hand.

"You see, we lucky we modern," said Chiong. "We almost free."

"Almost free?" I asked.

"Sure," she replied. "Only almost. Even a little girl like you know that."

Fishbite, who had gone to park the minivan, came in at this moment and huddled by the brazier.

"It's cold out there," he muttered. "Hi, Chiong. How's it been?"

"Okay. Good," Chiong said. She brought him a cup of the fragrant tea. "You Christmas good?" she asked him.

"Umhmm. Very good." He winked at me.

"I have dinner," she said, turning away and padding into the kitchen.

"Yeah, it was great. He debauched me," I called after her.

"Luck–" he began, and stopped as Chiong turned around.

"What?" she asked me, listening hard, clearly not identifying the meaning.

"Nothing," I replied and stared at Fishbite defiantly. I wasn't really going to tell her but I just wanted him to know that I could.

After dinner Chiong went home to the consulate and I sat on the opium couch for a long time, not wanting to move.

"Let's go up," Fishbite finally said. He had been reading the paper and was now finished with it.

"I'm going to sleep here," I said, and lay down in my clothes on the brocade cushion and closed my eyes.

"Let's go," he said, standing over me.

"I don't want to go up," I said, squirming away.

"I'll carry you," he offered, and when I shook my head, he added, "I'll just carry you up after you're asleep, you know."

"Yes. You're bigger and stronger than me," I replied angrily.

"I am," he said simply, and he picked me up and carried me, as I kicked at him violently, up the stairs and into my room, whereupon he set me down gently on the rug. He switched on the light, kissed me on the forehead, said, "Good night," and went out and closed the door behind him.

I was so relieved that my energy came flooding back and I sat up, excited to be home, and looked around. My dressing table was there, computer sitting on it, waiting for me to sit down. My stuffed animals—dolphin, elephant, bear, tiger, giraffe, shark, rabbit, owl—were piled as they'd always been along one wall and almost up to the ceiling. I never would part with any one of them, so they represented the stuffed animals of my entire life.

There was my little bed, a very plain and monastic single, with pink sheets, almost like a bed in a Barbie cell. The wall-to-wall carpeting was pink, the walls pink, the curtains pink, the lamp, a round globe in dusty rose.

And up on the wall over my bed, the Chinese poster my mother had given me: The Red Army of Women–the Cultural Revolutionary Ballet, featuring girls in army uniforms and toe shoes carrying guns.

I sat on the pink rug and stared around the room. Things were so different now. My mother and father were gone, both vanished in puffs of smoke. My stepdad was mentally sick. But maybe now that we were back, things would change again. Maybe he would stop and I would go on like I used to be. I'd just forget, like I did when I wasn't with him. It wasn't hard at all. I was glad to forget, so I did. Like that. Over. On to the next.

I went to the computer and sat down and signed on-line. There was mail, it turned out, from Eglantine Flout, who was still at Chutney.

"I've had the Perfect Fourteen," she wrote. "He was divine and so was IT. You must try IT soon!!!"

"Congrats! A warm hand on your opening!" I wrote back, stealing from, who was it–Noël Coward? Tallulah Bankhead? Robert Benchley? One of the old literates. They wrote that to someone in a play. I knew Eg would love it.

So Eg had had sex. That made me feel better, somehow. Not that I would ever have told her about Fishbite, even though she probably suspected. I was worried about going to foster care, and anyway, it's not the sort of thing you want people to know unless you've decided to go on a talk show and really discuss it. If and when I get my own show, I might talk about it then, like Oprah did–suddenly–when the viewers least expect it and when I could no longer be put some-place against my will. Then I would discuss it right out.

I left the computer and lay down on the rug. Sometime later I awoke, terrified. I stumbled from my room into the room that had been my mother's, and there before me was Fishbite, lying on the huge Chinese wedding bed. I crept into it next to him.

Perhaps it's shocking to you, Dear Readers and Watchers, shocking and incomprehensible that having finally been left alone, I would crawl back into the pervert's bed. If you must place blame, blame it on the cloth mother monkey, who is, you recall, better than no monkey at all.

13 I haven't written for a long time about the sex, and I am sure you are eager to know. We had been together now for about a month from the time Fishbite took me from Chutney, and no, Dear Readers and Watchers, nothing much had progressed. He had not forced himself on me, for reasons I thought were a form of pervert's honor or simple fear, but which I subsequently discovered were none of the above. At any rate, it was still oral sex, which the ancients called cunnilingus, or rabbit's tongue, as you know if you are good at languages, as I am.

Yes, it was still rabbit's tongue, which I was getting quite used to and which in its own peculiar way would end up ruining me for sex with other men anyway. For, according to the talk shows and despite protestations in the newspaper, rabbit's tongue is no more common among high school boys of the ending millennium, or any other age boys, than it has been for the previous one thousand years of male human history. And it does not promise to achieve prominence in the Asian-dominated high-tech world to come.

So I enjoyed it while I was forced to, and enjoyed forcing Fishbite to, and it amused me that we were both being forced to do it, and it was pretty confusing.

To this point, I had never touched Fishbite, absolutely refused to. And nightly he begged me for favors which I had vowed never to give.

"I want to teach you, Lucky," he would mewl. "When you grow up you must learn to be a good lover. I could teach you if you'd let me."

"No. I don't care. I don't want to know," I would reply petulantly. And I called the shots, for a while.

14 We set about our new life with pragmatic grace. Every night I slept with Fishbite, and every morning he would make me fix the bed in my room so that Chiong, who arrived in time to make breakfast, would suspect nothing.

I didn't feel like I minded doing this, but sometimes I would become so furious with the bedclothes that Chiong would find them strewn around my room, draping all and sundry.

"You a wild sleeper" was her only comment as I apologized.

In that first week, Fishbite had taken me by the hand to see the headmistress of Hatpin, my old school. He clothed his large body in tweeds that I had never seen before and, pipe in mouth, was posing as a literary man.

Mrs. Manly, the headmistress, did not see through him. We visited her office together, and it seemed to me that she was taken with him and was even flirting. He, on the other hand, writer or no writer, was shameless.

"Of course I've done most of my publishing in Italy and Japan," he lied. "I don't know why they like me there but they do."

"It's a global world, Mr. Fishbite," Mrs. Manly cooed. "You are lucky."

"Indeed," Fishbite said, to my astonishment. It sounded funny coming out of his mouth. He was so American.

"Just what is it you write about?" she asked, inclining her head his way and smiling sweetly. She was a solid, extremely white woman in her early sixties, a former gold medalist at dodgeball.

"The human condition, man's inhumanity to man, the coldness of our technological future, love . . ." he reeled off.

"Love?" she asked.

"Love," he repeated and nodded knowingly. "All kinds of love." He glanced my way. I rolled my eyes.

"We have a few writer parents, Mr. Fishbite," she said with obvious regret, "but not as many as in the past. Now we have more billionaires but fewer prose stylists. TV money. You understand?"

"Sadly," he said, "I do."

"But we have to keep the school running, don't we?" she asked.

He nodded.

"You look like an erudite man, sir," she went on. Fishbite nodded. I stifled a giggle.

"Then you of all people will appreciate how we feel about the end of the literate part of human history. This is, of course, reflected in the curriculum of Hatpin as, one by one, we drop Greek, Latin, and English for courses in 'anchoring the news desk in a crisis' and ever more esoteric computer programming. These sorts of endeavors are luring our mon-eyed young people these days. Perhaps you saw the news-paper piece—Harvard grads going into TV comedy?"

She tried but failed to avert the sneer that seized her fea-tures at the thought.

"Well," she sighed, "we like to think Chaucer still applies, at any rate."

"About Lucky Lady," Fishbite began.

"Of course she may return to Hatpin. As I recall, Lucky, your late mother got rid of the TV in favor of nightly recitals on that lilting Chinese instrument the *er-hu*, isn't that cor-rect, dear?" She turned her head to me. "I believe you still read?"

"Yes, ma'am," I replied. I did read now more than ever. Since I was back in my mother's house with Chiong, I was ploughing through her library on China. Chiong was instructing me in Mandarin. I was preparing for my place in the twenty-first century.

The only remnant of my connection with TV was my enduring love for the Disney Store.

The first day I was home, I rushed out and took the bus to visit the West Side branch. I walked in and everyone was nice to me, as always. I headed right for the Little Mermaid section. Basically I just liked touching the aqua plastic. It was so smooth. When I ran my fingers over it, it was like Greek worry beads—it instantly calmed me.

I liked the mugs, the backpack, the pencil case, and of course the clothes. I've worn a Little Mermaid bathing suit since I was six. My mother was against it, but I liked the mermaid so much I had to absorb some of her power if I could.

Ariel, the mermaid, seemed like such a cheerful girl. I still didn't really understand why she wanted to go up and live with humans, and especially marry a human man, when she had this calm underwater life. Her dad, Trident, seemed wonderful too—protective and powerful. Why make a dad like him angry at you? Why? For a guy who looks like a male model? I wouldn't. Not for anything.

But I trusted Ariel to do the right thing. She was strong enough was the answer. Secure enough. Not like me. I wasn't secure enough to give up a dad forever for a boyfriend. But that could be because I hadn't had a dad for so long.

"Lucky." I suddenly realized that Mrs. Manly was talking to me. "What did you do over Christmas?"

A picture popped into my mind of Fishbite naked at the Sheraton Flight Path looming over me.

I began to stutter. I had no idea what to reply. I felt Fishbite get nervous.

"We went skiing, Mrs. Manly, in Switzerland," he said. "Near Zermatt."

"How lovely." Mrs. Manly beamed. "When I was a girl we used to go there every spring. Did you have the raclette?"

Fishbite looked stumped.

"Delicious," I helped. "Though I prefer fondue."

I sat back, having saved the ruse, and sank into my chair. I felt terribly sad. I remembered coming here with my mother when we first came up from Texas. I remember how scared she was, and how I held her hand through the interview, not for me but for her. She was wearing a twenties look then, cloche hat, little short gloves, long thin silhouette, topped by her little thin nose and rosebud lips.

How ever did someone so delicate come to be mixed up with someone like Dad or Fishy, huge great puddings of men with giant skulls and jawlines and the souls of spineless boys? I could see their draw, of course—the sweet-naturedness, the puppylike devotedness, the goofy smiles. But what did she see in the fisheye part, the cold, calculating, self-aggrandizing, responsible-to-no-one untrustworthiness? She should have had better than that.

Tears of grief were cascading down my cheeks now, and I got Kleenex from my backpack and blew my nose.

"May I go to the bathroom, please?" I asked.

"Of course," they both responded and I left the room.

As I shut the door behind me, Mrs. Manly was saying, "I suppose some form of culture will persist as long as it has colored photographs."

15

I started cutting my legs up not long after I went back to Hatpin. It was lunch hour and I had brought the razor to school to shave my legs there, in the shower after gym, if I had time. It turned out I had time after lunch so I went to the shower room and when I started to put the new blade in the razor, I decided not to. Instead I just held it and sliced vertical patterns down my leg.

It didn't hurt, really, and it didn't bleed much. But it did make me feel bad, in the sense of cool-baaad. I was getting to the place where feeling baaad was at times very satisfying in a way that other things weren't. I also felt like I wanted to wear multiple earrings. My hormones were coming on strong.

16

It was hard to have a normal life with Fishbite on my case all the time. From the moment I messed up my bed in the morning until he put me into his bed at night, he monitored my whereabouts like a bodyguard. It was only after a good deal of pleading that Chiong got to walk me to school instead of him. I was the only thirteen-year-old girl in the world who was not allowed to walk to school alone.

It was not a matter of "them that fears it does it." He was not afraid of other molesters who might get me. Oh no. He was afraid of anyone who might befriend me. The man who ran the cleaner's and who had once given me candy was suspect, as was Mr. Avgolemono, who ran the diner and used to kiss me on the cheek when I went there with my mother.

Fishbite didn't trust my teachers, my friends, or my acquaintances. But curiously enough, he did trust Chiong, and so I was allowed to spend time with her and we did a lot together.

Every morning Chiong walked me to school and we breakfasted together at a giant bookstore, where we tried to improve her English by reading a prestigious newspaper.

She was always shocked at the amount of personal and sexual information that appeared in newspaper stories. I tried to explain the concept of sexual harassment, but she couldn't get it. She kept saying, "Like buying and selling girls?" to which I could only reply, "Oh no, not that bad," which, of course, confused her more. She couldn't understand how women could get money from men who mistreated them verbally on the job but not from the fathers of their children, which I told her confused me, too. "I think it's a matter of not being able to find the fathers," I told her, which she did understand, only too well.

In the afternoon, Chiong would wait for me outside the school and walk me up to the Metropolitan Museum, where we would take tea.

She loved the Egyptian Wing and would drag me by the hand to wander among the alabaster statuary and gaze at the tomb paintings.

She felt Ramses the Second was a full-blown paranoid because of the numerous statues of himself he had set up just about everywhere during his time. As far as she was concerned, he was trying to bribe the gods to be sure to get a good spot in the afterlife. Bribes, she confided, looking around to make sure no one was listening, were what had felled China once and would, she prophesied, fell China again.

She loved the statues and paintings of Akhenaton. She felt sorry for him because he was thought to have had dropsy. And she liked him because he was often depicted with his wife and children playing about at his feet. When she found out he worshiped one god, the sun god, that did it for her.

"A very nice man," she muttered, introducing him to other museumgoers passing by in the gallery. "Not like that Ramses."

After tea, we would walk back home—we always walked everywhere. (Chiong was used to walking miles and miles, as people are who live in Communist countries. Evidently, to Communists, one of the most luxurious parts of capitalist life is public transportation.)

And often Chiong would just start laughing. When I would ask why, she would nod to herself and reply that she was laughing out of joy—she had food, a nice place to live, a good job, and kind employers. America was everything it was cracked up to be and more.

Chiong taught me a lot. You would never find Chiong on a talk show. In her world, the tragedies of life were nothing to talk about. She wanted to talk about the good things as she saw them. She said the Chinese used to think that if you talked only of tragedy, the gods would not get jealous and so people made up tragedies to talk about.

That gave me the idea for a twenty-first-century show on which people would make up things that happened to them and talk about them. "My Sister Was Born with Two Heads and I Cut One Off When I Turned Three" was one topic I thought of. I don't know why. But I think it's a natural.

I didn't like it that Fishbite was controlling my social life, and I told him so. That only made him more suspicious. He made me carry a cell phone in my backpack so he could find me no matter where I was or what I was doing. And I often noticed him shadowing me when I was out walking with Chiong. I'd suddenly whip around just in time to catch him ducking into a doorway on Broadway or someplace, hat pulled down over eyes, like a spy in a French movie. Did I mention he sometimes reminded me of the French comedian Monsieur Hulot, only huskier? Well he did, not that he would have had any idea who that was.

And you know, it's funny, because up until that year, I don't think there's anyone I would have wanted to see more than my mother or Fishbite, the people in my family, anytime, anywhere. More than friends or anyone. But that year, I guess around the time I went to Chutney, I began to feel the opposite. It was just them I didn't want to see. Oklahoma bombing on East Eighty-third Street. Remember?

And sometimes when I'm very low I think, Did I wish my mom away? Did I do that? And then I realize no, I didn't–I couldn't have. But I just can't seem to keep a parent around me for longer than ten minutes, which is a bit of an exaggeration but not much.

After I left Chutney Eglantine Flout had returned to Hatpin. Her parents had heard about her doings with the Perfect Fourteen and made her come back to New York. We resumed our friendship, and when the school urged us to do some community service, we decided to do global service instead. Together we formed a political action group on behalf of the world's children. We called it WHINE!–World's Hapless Infants, Notice Everyone!–and our mission was to get attention paid.

But Fishbite forbade me to see Eglantine after school, along with everybody else, and that pretty much tore it for me, and for the first time in my life, I started lying about what I was doing.

I didn't lie to Chiong. No, she didn't deserve that. But when I went off with Eglantine I just told Chiong the exact location of where I would be and not whom I would be with.

"I come?" she would ask, looking worried.

"No, Chiong. It is all right. I'm going to the tearoom at the Plaza Hotel," I would answer. "I won't let Fishy know I was alone. You just go home to the embassy."

"But what if something happens?" Neither she nor I wanted her to lose her job.

"Nothing has happened at the Palm Court," I told her, "since *Eloise* was written in the 1950s. It's okay, really."

I always let Chiong walk me down Fifth Avenue to the Plaza on her way back to the consulate. The first time was the only time she timidly entered the hotel to have a look at the Palm Court tearoom.

"Ohhh," she sighed. "A little like the Peninsula Hotel in Hong Kong. So quiet. Okay. You can go here." And she went on home.

So every Friday afternoon when school ended early, Eg and I met in the Palm Court to discuss the life of children.

Potted palms and piano music, soft velvet armchairs and silver serving pieces. Little sandwiches and little sugar cookies. Even people who frequented the place knew the sort of life it represented was no more. Eglantine looked around and said, "I wish I lived at the turn of the century."

"Poor children were treated terribly then," I advised her.

"Then the thirties," she replied.

"What if you'd been a Jewish child in Nazi Germany?" I asked.

"Was there ever a time when all children were cared for?" she asked, exasperated.

"No. Did you see the paper today about child bondage?" I asked, getting down to business.

"Congress is passing a law?" she said.

"Yes, we won't import items made by children in bondage," I explained.

"I hope that's true," she said.

"Why haven't we done it up until now?" I wondered rhetorically.

"Because the children weren't white?" she offered.

"Quite possibly. Or people cared about money more," I said. "It is a step anyway," I added.

"All right," said Eg. "The sixth grader strangled going door-to-door raising funds for his school?"

"Someone kissed me once when I was going door-to-door for UNICEF," I told her.

"You were lucky, Lucky," she said.

"Poor kid. A murderous child got him. Poor both of them," I said.

"More and more child murderers these days?" asked Eg. "Or just more reported?"

"Both," I replied.

A muffled purr began emanating from my backpack beneath the table. Eg and I rolled our eyes in unison. It was Fishbite calling on the cell phone. I let it ring for a while just to upset him before I took it out and switched it on.

"Lucky?" he barked.

I panted loudly.

"Music?"

"I'm at ballet, remember? I really can't talk." I looked at Eg, who stifled a squeal.

"Later." He clicked off. He sounded like some guy out of a movie about the Marines.

I put my finger down my throat to indicate disgust to Eg.

I switched the phone off. "Modern technology has not liberated children at all," I said to Eg. "Okay, back to work—what are we doing this weekend?"

"We are going up and down Madison Avenue vandalizing Pike's Peak sneakers," said Eg.

"Right," I replied. "You are sure they are made by children in bondage?"

"Yes," said Eg. "I read it in this Internet newsletter on world labor infringements."

"Umhmm." I scanned the article in the newsletter and gave it back. "Okay. Anything else we should discuss?"

"We should do street theater about four-year-olds in rug factories chained to looms. I hate that so much, don't you?"

"Yes," I said, and we bowed our heads for a moment of silence.

"But it's a better life than being a four-year-old prostitute."

For a moment I wanted to tell Eglantine about me and Fishbite and the whole bag of snakes. For a moment, I identified with those little Thailanders ten times removed. I suddenly wanted to cry and scream and have one of my fits, and I wondered, did they have their fits too? What did they do to get their freedom out? What could little sex slaves do?

"Dear God," I said instead, and Eg and I bowed our heads again. "We pray for our little brothers and sisters in South Asia, and for the children who murder. Let them find some peace somehow. And if they die, take their little souls to heaven and for the first time in their lives, let them feel loved. Amen."

"Amen," said Eg.

And we drank the rest of our tea in silence, while the tinkling breeze from fluttering piano keys blew our velvet hair ribbons and calmed our unquiet thoughts.

17 When they asked me later what his body looked like naked, I couldn't tell them. I knew that he was very tall and fleshy and very white, uncannily like a giant pillow, but beyond that I never looked at him. I turned my head to the right as I lay on my back and closed my eyes tight. I surrendered to sensation because otherwise it would have been pain. A lot of children do. If he tried to kiss me or hug me, I just lay still and let him. Only if we were dressed and standing up did I ever kiss him back. Somebody had to draw a line somewhere.

18 On Saturday morning, Fishbite insisted on coming with me and Chiong to buy sneakers. I phoned Eg from the bathroom and alerted her to the problem. When we got to the store, Eg was trying on sneakers and we pretended to be surprised at seeing each other.

Fishbite was edgy. He stood right on top of me and Eg as we tried to talk until finally I had to push him away.

"Excuse me, I can't breathe," I told him.

"Sorry," he muttered.

"Did you bring the ink and eye droppers," Eg whispered.

"Yeah," I said and removed her set from my left pocket in my fist and slipped them onto the seat next to her.

I then rose up and went away from her.

"Nice to have seen you, Eg," I said as I moved away.

She nodded.

I walked over to the rack of children's sneakers and looked for the white boomerang that was the Pike's Peak logo. Every time I saw one, I'd pick up the sneaker and quickly drop several spots of India ink on the white leather or canvas, making an unremovable stain. Over in the adult department I could see Eg doing the same thing.

"Stop! What are you doing?" Fishbite's furious hiss singed my ear. "Come with me." He grabbed my hand and yanked me from the shop.

"Stop it!" I shouted at him, pulling away.

People stopped on the avenue and watched us. Fishbite was glowering with rage. Aware, however, of the sensation we were creating, he calmed himself and smiled a jaundiced smile.

"We'll speak when we get home," he muttered at me, and then, to himself, as he frogmarched me stiffly toward the house, "Can't even reprimand your child without committin' a crime."

I dragged my feet like a dog who doesn't want to brave the snow.

When finally we'd reached the house and he'd pulled me up the steps and into the living room, he gave vent.

"What the fuck were you doin'?" he screamed. "You could have been arrested! I could have been called into court–"

"And you know what my defense would have been?" I screamed back. "Abuse! In the home! Mother's boyfriend. The whole tired story!"

I threw myself on the couch, sobbing.

"What were you doing defacing other people's property like that?" he shouted.

I took a moment and decided not to tell him.

"Vandalism. Teenage vandalism among the privileged," I replied.

"Lucky." He softened his voice and got down on his knees before the couch. "You have to be very careful, sugar. You'll go right to a foster home if there's a problem. I won't be able to save you, hon'. And if this stuff keeps up, I won't try . . ."

I began to tune out here. I got a twist in my stomach and I felt so angry that I gritted my teeth and drew blood. I felt a drop of it slide out of my mouth and wet my lips.

"What's that? What's wrong?" Fishbite wiped the blood with his finger and then grabbed me and held me close. "Let's go upstairs and make up," he said, rising up off his knees and pulling me by the hand. I made myself a dead weight and forced him to carry me.

19 As a result of Fishbite's terror that we would be arrested, he said, his psoriasis returned with a vengeance and he went back to Dr. Naif's for more light treatments.

I saw him more and more often strolling down the avenue with Evie, and it began to make me angry. She was always trying to horn in on other people's experiences, primarily because she had so few of her own. Although she was arrogant from all her public exposure, it was no fun for her really. She was just another working child.

I didn't feel sorry for her, though. It was my Fishbite she was coveting, after all, and I didn't like it.

One day I bumped into her on the way home from school. Before I knew what I was doing, I backed her into a doorway and threatened her with a compass. Two big holes right in the dimples, I told her, and then went about my way. I felt weird about it afterwards, like someone else had done it, not me, and awfully, awfully sad. But that night, unless it was my imagination, I thought Fishbite came at me with renewed vigor.

Then for a time, with the exception of the sex stuff, everything was almost calm in my life. In the morning, Chiong came early and walked me to school. I was excelling there in Latin and geometry and looked to win a prize.

In the afternoon, Chiong picked me up and let me flirt at the bus stop with some boys from another private school. And this made me feel almost normal again. When the boys tried to snatch my books or talk to me about music, it was as if Fishbite had never existed. I was just another innocent girl, nervous about her effect and loving it.

I especially liked one boy, named Randolph Kennedy III, who was fond of putting his hand on my back and trying to feel my bra through my uniform. It was terribly exciting when he did this, his hot little hand almost burned through my blouse and I could hardly breathe.

It amazed me how much more thrilling this was than anything Fishbite was doing. Even the rabbit's tongue, which, they assure me here at the facility, is the number-one woman-pleaser, gave me only so much pleasure. But then, I didn't want to like it, and maybe that was what was really the matter.

My friendship with Chiong, who treated me like the child I was, became closer and closer. She told me about her life, which had been very hard.

Her parents had been persecuted during the Cultural Revolution, and at the age of three, she had been sent, of necessity, to an orphanage in her home province. It was because of the poor nutrition she received there that she had lost several of her teeth. I forced Fishbite to pay for her cosmetic dentistry, one of the few things from that time of which I remain proud. And to his credit, he did it with grace. Or maybe it was just that I was getting meaner and he was getting afraid.

Chiong had been reunited with her parents about ten years later, but by that time, she said, their spirits had been broken as well as their health. She went to work at thirteen, the age I was then, to support her family by making and selling dumplings from a wagon in the street. She was working at the wagon when she met her future husband, the diplomat.

They fell in love instantly, she said. And when he learned that her parents were both doctors, albeit invalided, he was overjoyed. There would have been no way for him to marry a street vendor, he had confided. Even the Communists couldn't bridge that class distinction.

They had a son, but he was back in China with his father's parents. The child was a musician, she told me proudly, a master of the *er-hu* at the age of eight, invited to play in Beijing for the country's leaders on state occasions.

She showed me pictures of Joe, as she called him, intently playing the Chinese violin, his little closed eyes like pencil lines drawn carefully on his face.

"Don't you miss him?" I asked once. "Aren't you angry that the government keeps him in China?"

"I would be angry at my whole life if I start," she replied. "Why bother? I miss him like the earth misses water in a drought. But now I play with you, okay?"

20 Sometimes, on a bus or at school or in the street, I would hear the word "mother" and my throat would close and tears would line up in my eyes like soldiers on guard against an advancing enemy. I couldn't talk. I couldn't think. The pain of missing her was so great I thought I'd crack.

Sometimes I would try to imagine her in a corner of the living room, perched on one of those teakwood swan-backed Chinese chairs, telephoning to an antique store, as she so often did.

"Mama," I would squeak out to this apparition of my sorrow, "can you forgive me? Please forgive me."

But she refused to look at me and all she would say was "Jack Daniel's and Shirley Temple–doesn't that say it all?"

21 The irony was that in this period, although he phoned me constantly, I hardly saw Fishbite. He wasn't awake when I went to school with Chiong in the morning and he wasn't home when she walked me back at three in the afternoon.

Once, I thought I saw him loitering outside the Dodger Academy where Evie Naif went to school, round about pick-up time, but I wasn't sure until later, of course, when the whole shoddy business was brought to light.

But he wasn't at my house, that's all I knew. He was just a disembodied voice on the cell phone, barking one-word greetings, jerking our mutual collars. Sometimes, long after dinner, he would run in, freshly showered, in time, as he put it, to tuck me into bed.

"Where have you been?" I asked him one night when I had been especially lonesome all day.

"I'm doing research for a novel," he said, "a great novel. One that will make my name."

"What's it about?" I asked, interested. He rarely showed enthusiasm for anything.

"I can't say until it's written," he replied darkly. "It will take away my spontaneity."

"Please give me a hint." I grabbed his lapels and mewed like a kitten. He always liked that.

"The fashion business and the future of Man," he said curtly. "That's the best I can do right now."

"Are you going to fashion shows?" I prodded. "Did you see supermodels? Do I really look like Kate Moss, as Randolph Kennedy says?"

Fishbite went silent and peered at me strangely.

"Who's Randolph Kennedy?" he asked with a menacing tone.

"A boy," I said sulkily. "A boy who likes me."

I enjoyed seeing the panic in his eyes.

He was about to say something but he stopped himself.

"What?" I said. "What?"

"Nothing," he replied. "Nothing."

22 Eglantine and I continued our WHINE! meetings on Fridays at the Plaza Hotel. We were extremely proud of having pulled off our first terrorist act, and we even made it into the newspapers, as Eg had left our manifesto in one of the sneakers announcing our intentions:

We are the members of WHINE!–World's Hapless Infants, Notice Everyone!–an organization which insists the world take note of its hapless infants and change their situation. That means you, Pike's Peak sneaks! You employ child labor at dirt-cheap wages in South Asia and you know it. We will ink your sneaks until you stop!

"Hmm," mused Eg. "They have our description–look here."

I read what she was reading: " 'Two teenage girls, about five feet four, both blond, slender, wearing black Ninja outfits . . .' Ninja outfits? Where did they get that?"

"We live in a time when salesgirls on Madison Avenue can't tell Armani when they see it." Eg shook her head. "Shame."

"They put in the Ninja outfits to make us out to be scary teenagers. Unbelievable," I said. "But Pike's Peak has been embarrassed. That's the main thing."

We toasted each other with teacups.

"All right now," I said, getting down to new business, "are we building the bomb?"

"Yes," said Eg. "I downloaded the instructions from a white supremacist's website last night. Here they are."

She handed me a printout on which was a very simple recipe, which I won't write here in case children are reading this. It was so simple that I scoffed at first.

"Horse manure?" I said sarcastically, mentioning one of the ingredients listed.

"Central Park–there's plenty of it. Look, we don't want a remake of the World Trade Center. We want an explosion that will get noticed and not harm anyone."

Our intention was to bomb the German Airlines office at night to protest the number of Germans who traveled to Thailand to have sex with children. We had gathered together a lot of facts about this and we felt it was time to act.

"I wouldn't have wanted to have sex without wanting to," Eg said softly.

"No. You wouldn't," I inadvertently snapped.

"What's wrong?" she asked me.

I reread the bomb-building instructions she had given me to divert her attention. As I did so, I realized the rashness of our endeavor.

"I'm not sure about a bomb," I said.

"Why not?" she asked.

"It's too much, you know, and not enough," I replied. "The people who will really suffer are police, firemen, and the insurance company for the airline. No. No. If we wish to publicize the children's plight, I say we use street theater, starring ourselves and anyone from our class who wants to help us."

"Great idea." Eg beamed. "It's just the thing for the war criminal's daughter—what's her name? She'll love it!"

"Keema Thep. She's very wild. She was never allowed to leave the palace until her dad made a run for it." I knew this from Chiong, who made it her business to know about the Asians at my school. "She didn't know how to button a button until she was ten years old."

"Wow," said Eg. "Didn't she want to know?"

"No. She never saw her mom"—it was an effort to get that word out. I stuttered it and limped on—"button a button. Why should she want to?"

"No, but we saw our moms drink and we don't want to," argued Eg.

"Yet. Give it time, Eg. We still have college ahead of us. There's still time for a drinking problem. Listen, street theater with all of us in costume in front of the German Consulate first, then move it to the Japanese Consulate, and the Consulate of the Netherlands?" I paused to get my breath. I was terribly excited by the thought of it. "What do you think?"

"Keema Thep. Think of the publicity! Brilliant, what else could I think?" smiled Eg.

23 My lawyer, Ms. Velvet Glove, whom Chiong found for me after the event, wants me to let you know, Dear Readers and Watchers, that as I went about setting up the performance, the pressure in my head was building.

I really feel, looking back, that I got involved so deeply in the performance precisely because Fishbite was home so little and I was so lonely. Perhaps it was to get his attention, which it did—how could he miss it?

The true crime, as I've said before, of the Manageable Molesters is that they wouldn't know love if it came up and kissed 'em. You can quote me on that. It's a sound bite.

Anyway, at home I was quite furious. Enraged, really. Chiong said I would have made a great Red Guard when she saw me destroy my room one day when I came home early and Fishbite wasn't there again. It was thanks to her that I didn't tear out my hair.

I was lying on the carpet in a flying debris of paper, feathers, glitter, and old stuffed animals. I was beginning to yank at my scalp when she rushed in.

"Stop," she said, holding my hands. "You too sad. Don't hurt self."

I started to sob hysterically. She put her arms around me and wept too.

After a time, she got up and started to pick up the mess.

"Don't bother," I said.

"You help me," she replied. "Together we bother. Always bother," she added. "Make meaning when there is none."

Some hours later, as I was drifting off to sleep, Fishbite appeared and sat on the bed.

"Where have you been?" I asked.

"Light treatments," he replied. "Then I had dinner with the Naifs."

"Why didn't you call?" I peered sadly at him through my tangled hair.

"I did. I called the house phone. Didn't Chiong tell you?" For a moment I got furious with her. Then I realized he was lying. I wondered why he didn't know I knew it.

"No," I replied softly. "Why aren't you home in the afternoon when I get home anymore?"

He looked terribly guilty. After a moment or two of deep thought, he said, "The light treatments cost a fortune, darlin'. In return, hon', as sort of a barter thing, I offered to sit with Evie and defray some of their nanny costs."

"What?" I sat upright and snarled like a dog. I was this close to biting him. As it was, I bared my teeth and hissed. He drew back.

"What's wrong?" he yelled defensively. "She's a child."

I screamed.

"No! Don't baby-sit!"

"Be reasonable, Lucky," he said. He was standing now on the other side of the room with a terrified look on his face but his voice was oily and unctuous. "We're running out of money. Your mother drank most of hers up. Hatpin costs a fortune. Chiong isn't free. I need the treatments. I need them."

I calmed the part of me that he could see, and he returned to the bed and stroked my brow. He didn't know that inside I was all steam and swirling.

"Relax, sugar," he murmured. "You're the only girl I'll ever love." He caressed me with the softest hands I've ever felt, the hands of a healing angel.

Too bad they were attached to the arms of a lying skunk.

24

It was after that that I threw myself into the performance with total abandon.

Eg and I worked together writing the script, and we enlisted the acting talents of Keema Thep, Inharmonia Chen, daughter of the Hong Kong multimillionaire importer, and Sondra Kowtower, daughter of the software billionaire art collectors.

I grant you, Dear Readers and Watchers, that each of these girls had an ax to grind. Inharmonia's father was a terrible disciplinarian and slapped her face with a regularity that indicated sadism. Sondra's parents were always in the columns and were known to be classless celebrity-sucks, which totally shamed her. And then of course there was Keema, whose dictator father had slaughtered millions and drained a country's coffers, myself, and Eg, who was simply old Southampton WASP and was neglected and bored. We were an explosion waiting to happen.

Our main problem, of course, in creating street theater about the sex industry in Thailand, was what to do about the male aspect. Should we include men in the script, exclude them, play them ourselves, get boys to play them, what?

They were certainly the raison d'être. Did our hatred of male tourists' indifference to the suffering of children require that we satirize or inform them? If we left them out and had a sex slave slumber party, where was our drama?

As Eg and I were studying Greek tragedy at Hatpin, we saw the playlet as containing a lot of ululating (from the Greek, meaning "to wail in kind of a rhythmic shriek"). We could easily make Greek tragic masks for all the characters. Eg and I went back and forth trying to figure this out.

In the end, Eg and I decided to have men in the script and to hire real male adult actors to play them. Inharmonia paid their salaries out of her enormous allowance, and we held auditions at Sondra's parents' house on East Seventieth Street while they were away at the Venice Biennale.

Sondra, a skinny blonde with big blue eyes, braces, and an evil, cackling laugh, called up all the agents in town and gave them our description of the parts: "Lascivious men in their late forties through fifties, straight and gay."

She told them we were an NYU student film project with a grant from the National Endowment for the Arts. At the appointed time and day, Sondra's townhouse doorstep was mobbed with middle-aged men looking for their big break.

A few of them, all fathers, to their credit, read our script, found their parts reprehensible, and left. But many many others found the roles "challenging," "a relief from the usual pablum," "Oscar-nomination characters."

In part, their enthusiasm was due to the media interest Sondra was so deftly creating around our project. We wanted every major network, CNN, and all the city's newspapers to be on hand for the playlet we would perform outside the three consulates.

According to our plan, we would go from one to another, gathering a crowd as we went. The playlet would begin at ten in the morning in front of the German consulate, move to the Japanese consulate, and end at the consulate of the Netherlands at eleven-thirty. The playlet itself would last about fifteen minutes and, we hoped, would be unavoidable. We were in the best position theatrical artistes could be in— we did not care about good reviews; it was arrest and notoriety we were seeking.

By the end of the day, we had found our tourists. We hired Gert Lichen, a huge German man in his early fifties whose very presence symbolized Bavaria; Bobby Hall, a lanky American gay man in his early forties with a cynical and sarcastic delivery; Gen Kroka, a Japanese man in his late forties with a cold, steely glance; and Martin Crisp, an entirely nondescript midwestern type in his fifties, the colorless type of man people are shocked to find molests or mass murders. They were all perfect. Eg and I were thrilled.

To allay his suspicions, I told Fishbite that I was having weekly playdates with Sondra Kowtower (not so far from the truth), and, as intended, he was ridiculously impressed. Of course he knew of the Kowtower Collection through his mother's gallery, and he had told me when he read Hatpin's parents list that he desperately wanted to meet them and flog some of her mule paintings to them. It was a sad fact that the eighties were over. Her pictures had lost all of their value.

To be honest, his hunger for the Kowtowers was the main reason I asked Sondra to be involved. There were other girls in the class with better media connections, daughters of network heads and the like, but Sondra was for Fishbite. I let her answer the cell phone when he called repeatedly during rehearsals, and she told me she liked his voice a lot. In fact, all the girls came to love him.

"He's so succinct and he cares about you so much," they would gush, which, as you know, Dear Readers and Watchers, was a gross and pathetic misunderstanding of the actual situation.

So Sondra fed items to the columns, and rehearsals began. We held them at Inharmonia Chen's. The second floor of her house had a ballroom, and her parents were away in Korea making deals to export grain so the North Koreans could eat. She paid the maids in her house to keep quiet about us and to entertain Keema's bodyguards, and everything ran smoothly.

About the third week of rehearsals, we had a big break. Sondra's parents had the big TV anchor Madge Froth and the reporter Barbara "Pecky" Peckworth to dinner.

As Sondra was seated between them, she was able to hand out our press releases to them personally and discuss the plight of children enslaved in the sex industry in Thailand. When Sondra's mother realized Sondra was monopolizing the two women's attention, she sent her up to bed with weak excuses about school. But not before Sondra had shamed both women into taking note of the playlet and had mentioned Keema Thep's starring role.

In fact, our playlet was just the media bombshell both women had been looking for, both to assuage their guilt for the cushiness of their lives and to reinvigorate their careers. Together they embraced us as their number-one cause.

It is ample proof of his distraction at that time that Fishbite failed to notice any references to us in the columns. Not that he knew of WHINE!, but where he actually was on the days that Eg and I were mentioned by name, I can only now guess. If he was writing a novel, it was never found. He could have been at the Ten Freedoms Spa in Chinatown, but I will tell about that later. The point is, though he was in constant contact with us on the cell phone, he missed our publicity. The first he heard of WHINE! was when the police phoned him from the Midtown South precinct. But I am getting ahead of myself.

Chiong made the costumes. I had explained the purpose of the playlet to her and she had offered to do it, gratis.

She had learned to make costumes after the Cultural Revolution, she told me, as another way to earn money to eat.

Her mother had lost her eyes during a struggle meeting that got out of hand, and her father had tried to commit suicide by jumping from a window; he had survived but was unable to walk properly. When she was reunited with them after the revolution was over, and found they could not, as she had dreamed, take care of her, she had to find more employment besides the dumpling wagon to care for them.

In the evenings after she finished selling dumplings, she apprenticed herself to a costumer from the Peking Opera and learned to sew. Now she designed and executed sex-slave outfits for us that were so sexy and yet so adorably modest that they brought tears to people's eyes. Our costumes were made from tattered and tarnished pink tulle and glitter. Little princesses in shreds, with here and there a waist, a leg, a shoulder, an ankle, bared. Around our necks and heads and waists, the most delicate of black chain jewelry. Our ankles were chained together too, making it painful and slow to walk. How we dragged our little bodies was enticing and agonizing all at once.

Our torn and stained pink undershirts had little bows, a poignant touch, we thought; the rips were not prurient but exposed only the boniest of little ribs.

After rehearsing for three weeks, we were ready. It was part of the media hype that we would announce the date of the happening only when we were ready so the anticpation would build, and build it had.

It was now the middle of February, but as our luck would have it, a warm spell came over the city. Temperatures rose into the fifties and throngs of sun worshipers filled the streets. It was time to strike.

I remember waking up the morning of the event in a state of sheer delight, only to discover that for some reason Fishbite was home. He importuned me as Chiong was ringing the doorbell, which almost put a damper on my spirits. But I rushed from his bed into my room, rumpled the bed quickly, and took a shower.

When I came out, I peeked into his bedroom and saw Fishbite watching MTV. He had become a fan of a girl group from England called the Vice Girls, primarily, I thought, because of the skintight costumes they wore. Though most of the time this made me furious, that particular morning I was glad of his preoccupation. I closed the door to my room and phoned Eg.

We had paid the assistant art teacher at school to construct a giant loom out of plywood, to which all of us would be chained by papier-mâché chains and locks. Though the loom had nothing to do with the sex industry, we were so stricken with the image of four-year-old Indian rug makers chained to looms that we had to use it. We were to pick it up by one of those jeep taxis at nine-thirty that morning.

"Eg?"

"Yes." Eg was whispering, which usually meant her step-father was home from the office with gout.

"Did you phone Miss Polles? Is it ready?"

"Ready and waiting," she replied.

"Talk to Sondra and Inharmonia?"

"Roger. I can't get through to Keema," Eg said. "I hope she shows up."

"She will," I assured her. "It's her one chance at redemption right now. See you in forty minutes."

Carefully I put on my costume and over it, an old raincoat. I went into the bathroom and patted on the most dolly of makeups until I looked adorable; then I streaked my face with fake dirt from the makeup store until I looked adorable, haunting, and poignant.

I crept down the stairs and into the kitchen, where Chiong was awaiting my appearance. She sucked in her breath when she saw me and then came over to examine my makeup.

"Very real," she said with obvious admiration and shook her head from side to side at the strangeness of it all.

Chiong was coming with us. When we had explained to her what we were doing, she had approved wholeheartedly. The idea of political street theater thrilled her to her marrow. The plight of poor children in Asia, and especially little girls, was something she knew intimately. Because of the delicate circumstances–her work with the Chinese government–she would not be able to take part. She would stand off to the side, guarding us surreptitiously, but looking as if she were an innocent bystander.

Quickly I grabbed my backpack and took her by the hand, and we fled out the front door down to the street. I ran with her until we were far enough away to escape Fishbite, and luckily we were able to commandeer a jeep taxi, which we directed to the Hatpin School.

Miss Polles was waiting with Eg out front, along with a papier-mâché loom approximately four feet square. Miss Polles was wide-eyed and ethereal, an artist of the New Age. She worshiped the Mother goddess and was a disciple of a female guru from India, which she said were her raisons d'être for getting involved with us, but in truth she was from Iowa and had no idea what we were getting her into.

The taxi driver helped us maneuver the loom into the spacious back of the jeep taxi. He was from Pakistan and was intrigued by the beauty of the fake loom.

"Did you ever see children rug makers chained to looms?" I asked him. Since we were on our way to protest, I took the chance and got up the nerve to inquire.

"Oh, yes," he said softly. "But then," he added, "I have seen much worse than that."

I glanced at Eg and a pall fell over us. There was something about the finality of what he said that reminded us of the seriousness of our mission and deflated our enthusiasm. We rode in silence to the German consulate. It was only seeing Inharmonia and Sondra standing there, anxiously awaiting our arrival, that rekindled our energy. We got out, paid the man, and invited him to stay for the performance. He almost did, but when he saw the interest we were creating in the embassy police guards, he got back into the taxi and drove away.

We carried the loom to the patch of sidewalk just in front of the entrance to the consulate, blocking the way. Gert Lichen, Gen Kroka, Bob Hall, and Martin Crisp rushed up to greet us. Gert was carrying the little machine that was their prop. They were all perfectly attired in the nondescript garb of the middle-class male tourist. To a man they looked drab.

Just as the guard began to emerge from the little cubicle he sat in, I laid my backpack on the pavement to one side and began to center myself, Hart-like. At that moment,

Keema's limo drew up and out she sprang, in costume, followed by her two bodyguards. They were large, burly Asian men wearing dark glasses and carrying walkie-talkies. Keema ran to us and together, as rehearsed so many times, we five girls immediately chained ourselves to the weaving machine by means of little locks that actually worked.

We were now a rather large human-and-papier-mâché object. Moving us was now no easy task. The guard stopped in his tracks and stared at us, bewildered. Then the cell phone in my backpack began to ring.

During this strange moment in the proceedings, a taxi arrived and out popped Madge Froth and Pecky Peckworth. Their taxi was followed by a van with camera crane on top and an entourage of newsmagazine employees. They arranged themselves quickly and expertly around us and began shooting. Madge and Pecky took up microphones on opposite sides of the "stage," and as they began narrating into them, a man who was probably the director shouted, "Wait! Where is that ringing phone? Could someone get it?"

One of Keema's bodyguards tore open the backpack and answered the phone. I couldn't believe he was doing it.

"And who the fuck are you?" I heard him snarl at Fishbite before he hurled the phone into the street.

"Out in front of the German consulate today," took up Pecky, "the tragedy of child sexual exploitation was enacted by five scantily clad preteens from the Hatpin School, among them the daughter of deposed president and South Asian mass murderer Bloody Thep."

"Their undershirts torn, their little ribs showing, their dolly faces smeared with dirt, the five Hatpin scholars tore into the soft underbelly of the child sex industry in Thailand. The Germans were their first target," began Madge.

Ululating above the din, we began our playlet. Each of us was chained to a part of the loom, and we all were kneeling and keening. Four of us were girls, clad in ripped pink tulle and glitter. One (Sondra) was a boy, in a black Chinese pajama outfit. All of us children had numbers on placards around our necks. The adult men stood in a line in front of a little number machine such as one sees at a bakery. As the play began, each man took a number.

"I've got number one," shouted Gert heartily.

I was one. I hung my head.

"Two," shouted Bob Hall. Sondra, the boy, cringed.

"Forty-five," shouted Martin Crisp. Eg slumped her head to her knees.

"Fifty," shouted Gen Kroka, and Keema wailed.

"The chest numbers," intoned Pecky, "are actually used in child brothels in Thailand, even further reducing children to nonperson status."

She had gotten this fact from the press release Sondra had given her at her parents' dinner party. It was true. They put numbers on the kids. But there wasn't a bakery machine. That was our addition, for art's sake. The men just chose the child they wanted by its number.

"Taking a number to violate a child? Can there be anything colder?" Madge addressed the camera. This report was the best thing she'd ever done.

Gert walked over and roughly kissed me. Crisp kissed Eg. Hall kissed Sondra. Kroka slapped Keema. The crowd gasped. The guard spoke urgently into his telephone.

"Come here, you little slut," shouted Gert and slapped me down to the pavement.

"Now you fuck me, bitch," screamed Crisp and climbed over Eg.

"Show me your ass," said Bob, and yanked down Sondra's pants, revealing jockey shorts.

Keema screamed at Kroka with pain: "No, no, please, mister. Mommy. Mommy."

We went for the hard stuff. Because that's the way it was. Men being their most brutally sexual with little kids who couldn't get away. The crowd on Park Avenue was horrified by the vulgarity, though they heard the words on TV and in movies all the time.

It was that we children were so heartrending that got them. Inharmonia was as beautiful as a Chinese movie star, a living rosebud, of tiny stature, and when she cried, the audience cried too. Out of Keema and Sondra and all of us came the real pain of moral children forced to live under morally indifferent grown-ups. It was this communal agony that chained us together, not a bunch of papier-mâché links.

Perhaps some were titillated by our playlet. One thing I've learned is there's always a molester in the crowd. But the men hadn't even started to whip us when the police cars, sirens blaring, drove up. They smashed right over Fishbite's cell phone, which, against all odds, suddenly started ringing again.

Pecky and Madge were so delighted, they could hardly keep somber. A melee ensued, in which Keema's bodyguards tried to carry her off and into the limo but couldn't because she was chained to the loom, as were Sondra, Eg,

Inharmonia, and I. We shrieked as we were dragged painfully across the pavement after her. Chiong started to run to our aid, but the police cut her off, went to grab the loom, and were attacked by the bodyguards. There was a terrible fight, during which two policemen were injured and we girls cowered on the pavement, watching men hurt each other and knowing it was our fault. It was only when some mounted policemen galloped down Park Avenue to assist us that horses trampled the cell phone and Fishbite was finally silenced.

When the bodyguards were subdued and the fight was over, we five Hatpinnies, still chained to the loom, were arrested and carried to a police van in a tangled mass, to be taken to the Midtown South precinct. Chiong ran after us. She was terribly afraid for me and risked being sent back to China to stay by my side, but I knew that Madge Froth and Pecky Peckworth would get us off, so as they pulled me into the police van, I told her to go back to the Chinese consulate, and, reluctantly, she went.

The police questioned us for hours. In protest, we refused to give our names, but eventually they got them from Hatpin. It was not until five that afternoon that they finally reached Fishbite.

It was an unctuous man in a pinstripe suit who entered Midtown South and identified himself as the stepfather and guardian of one Lucky Lady Linderhoff.

I had never seen Fishbite dressed that way before. He looked like an investment banker. On his feet were wing tips. His collar was starched white atop a blue striped shirt. His cuff links were solid gold. His blond hair was slicked back from a clean-shaven face ruddy with what seemed to me to be my mother's Dior rose blush. He carried an expensive leather briefcase.

I was sitting on a bench near the desk sergeant's desk, cut papier-mâché chains still dangling from my ankles, wrist, and waist. He came up to me and stared into my eyes.

"Lucky, what on earth, dear?" he said with a fake lockjaw accent of the type associated with Yale. He sounded concerned but his glance was flat with rage. He looked so rich that the police gazed at him with respect.

"We were trying to make a point, Stepdad," I said, staring back. It was eerie. I couldn't see the man I knew in him at all.

At this moment, the precinct doors swung open and in hurried a sleek-looking Asian man followed by an entourage of scary-looking Asian thugs in dark glasses. Clearly this was Keema's dad, the deposed president and war criminal. He rushed up to the desk sergeant and began to deal with the arrest of his bodyguards. Of course they had diplomatic immunity and would immediately be released. But the police had conveniently lost their identification in order to keep them in cells for a while to punish them for their violence.

Keema was sitting on the bench with me, and she wept when she saw her father. He did not acknowledge her at all until he had finished arranging for his guards' release.

Only then did he turn and say something in their language, a quick, high-toned machine-gun spurt, after which she fell to her knees before him and begged forgiveness. Since I had just witnessed Inharmonia Chen's dad slapping her face when he thought no one was looking, I felt a lot more comfortable in Fishbite's custody than I otherwise would have. And of course I had never seen him as a banker before—the getup somehow endowed him with an unexcitability that looked comforting even if it wasn't real.

"Well," Fishbite droned to the detective as they released me formally, "it was for a good cause anyway. Kids today!"

"Yeah." The detective, a seasoned New York guy with a Queens accent, looked at him closely. "You're the sole surviving parent here?" he asked. Drops of sweat stood up and saluted on the back of Fishbite's neck.

"Yes," he moaned ruefully, as if he cared. "Yes. My wife, Lucky's dear mother, was killed in a car accident on Madison Avenue several months ago."

"The hit-and-run?" The detective said. He was picking up a scent. His ears twitched almost like a dog's. Fishbite nodded. He seemed dead calm all of a sudden.

"Boxer Rebellion Antiques?" the detective asked, interrogating now.

I jumped forward. "Yes. Yes. Do you know anything? Do you?" I cried out, and grabbed his arm to get his attention.

He stared at me kindly. "No," he replied softly. "We don't, honey. Except the driver was a big guy, big." He fixed his gaze on Fishbite, who turned toward the door.

"Let's go, Lucky," he said sweetly, shepherding me out onto the street. He turned back once to add, "Call us, Detective, if you get something. We need some closure."

As soon as we were out the door, Fishbite dropped my hand and fled down the steps in the direction of our house. A rush of photographers pounded after us. Fishbite did not look back at me. He hurtled down the street. He seemed to have forgotten about me entirely. I ran to catch up with him.

"I know you're angry but it was important," I said, running beside him.

He didn't look at me or speak. As a photographer caught up with him, he took a pair of dark glasses from his pocket and donned them.

"I can't say I'm sorry," I said, breathless now from our pace. "Getting arrested was the intention, though not to scare you."

He gave no indication that he had heard me. He was totally preoccupied, thinking intently about something and thinking fast.

"Fishy?" I wanted to see if he was hearing me. "Fishy!" I shouted. He jerked to consciousness and glanced my way. He looked confused and scared, almost vulnerable.

"What?" he asked, his Texan drawl returning.

"Aren't you going to say anything to me, bawl me out or anything?" His reaction, or lack of it, was making me terribly uneasy. I began to shake a little.

"There's nothing to say," he replied, and spotted a free cab and hailed it. The photographer snapped us as we bundled into it and sped away.

Fishbite leaned back against the seat, closed his eyes, and sighed. I looked out the window at the lit-up storefronts that raced by as we shot up Madison Avenue. Usually they comforted me but not tonight. Tonight they made me feel lonely and scared and way on the outside of things. I began to shake violently now, as if I were in shock.

Fishbite took no notice.

I was still shaking hard when finally we had made our way up the front stoop and were inside our house. Fishbite made no move to help me. Keeping his silence, he climbed the stairs, went into the bedroom, and shut the door with a slam.

My head was all jumbled up. Our playlet was a great success but I felt terrible. Froth and Peckworth had filmed the melee and rushed off, thrilled. I hadn't even thought about Fishbite through most of it. I just assumed he would be angry, like Keema's dad or Inharmonia's. (Sondra's and Eg's parents had sent the nannies, which meant they were too mortified to even come.)

I couldn't figure out what was going on. But I felt so sad that I didn't even turn on the news. I tried to phone Eg, but her line rang and rang, which meant it was unplugged. I drank some milk and slowly climbed the stairs. When I went to open the bedroom door and see what Fishbite was thinking, I couldn't. He had locked it.

25 In the morning I awoke in my room around nine o'clock, late for me, and realized that it was the first time in months that I'd slept through the night. No one had waked me and wanted things from me. I felt strangely free.

The light filtered in through the snow-white curtains and a little patch of gold was lit up on the dark coverlet like a sudden squirt of sun on a cloudy sea. I had forgotten that this happened, this little miracle of light. My mother used to say maybe the builder of our house planned it that way, like the Mayans planned the little square of light that appears in Mayan temples on the solstice.

I got up and peered into the bedroom, but Fishbite wasn't there, watching MTV. The bed was rumpled. The closet doors stood open and inside there was nothing except for my mother's clothing, which none of us had touched. Fishbite's clothes and bags were gone.

I ran down the stairs and into the kitchen. Chiong was at the sink, watching the morning news on a tiny TV.

"You not on," said Chiong, perplexed. "Why not?"

"Have you seen Stepdad?" I asked. I was frantic. I rushed down the steps to the garden as I heard her call, "No. Have not seen him."

I pressed my face to the glass window of the downstairs apartment and surveyed his office. The drawers were pulled open and were empty. The big roll of paper was gone, the short stories no longer in their place in the "out" box.

Shivering with cold, I ran back upstairs in time to hear Chiong answer the ringing phone.

"Eglantine. How are you today? You all right?" She handed me the phone.

"Eg. We're not on? Not in the papers? Did you call Sondra? I see."

It was, according to Sondra, a news blackout. Froth and Peckworth would not confess whether it was the Hatpin School or Keema's dad, the war criminal (now heavily involved with the CIA), who had called in favors, but the two women had been told to shelve the story and the city's newspapers had gone silent on us too.

"Amazing," I told Eg. "Actually, I'm impressed."

"I'm in a lot of trouble over here–how about you?" whispered Eg. "My phone's been yanked out. I'm talking on Mom's cell now. She's in the shower."

I suddenly got very nervous when she reminded me. "Fishy seems to be gone," I said very softly so that it might not be true.

"What do you mean 'gone'?" she asked. She sounded concerned, which scared me more.

"Clothes gone. Office cleaned out." I said this matter-of-factly to try to get control of it.

"You're kidding," said Eg. This seemed very serious to her.

"It's fine," I said quickly. "He'll be back. He's just teaching me a lesson or something. He's not a parent. He doesn't know that scares a child."

Eg didn't reply. I could hear her thinking. Finally she said, "I'll see you at school. We're not allowed to play together for a while. And I'm grounded for three months. But it was worth it, wasn't it?"

"Not if we didn't get any publicity, it wasn't," I snapped. "We should have made the bomb."

"Next time," said Eg, and we both hung up, laughing.

26 For the first week after Fishbite was gone, I wandered through the house from room to room, from top to bottom, and awaited his return. Looking back, I would say I was terrorized, really, struck silent with pain.

I didn't go to school. I wasn't capable of it. I spent countless hours sitting at the living-room window, staring into the street, hoping to see him lumber up the stairs to the front door.

But he didn't come and he didn't come. And slowly but surely, the groceries ran out, and then the money that he left in a teapot for Chiong to spend on the household.

At first, I suppose, she assumed he was on a short trip, back by the weekend, the usual working affair. But as she watched me and saw the supplies diminish and my panic rise, she no longer trusted her instinct.

At the end of that first week, she finally questioned me. "Where's your stepfather?" she asked in her blunt way.

I burst into tears.

"What's the matter?" she asked soothingly, cradling me in her arms.

"He seems to be gone," I managed.

"Gone?" she repeated hesitantly.

"Gone," I repeated back. "I think forever."

She said nothing for a moment, pondering this.

"But he's your stepfather. You have no one else." She said this as if Fishbite had defied all logic.

My throat was full of tears. I could not reply.

"Do you have money for yourself?" She sounded angry now, not, I could see, for herself but for me.

"No," I got out. I cleared my throat. I felt hot and feverish from grief. "Maybe there's some in some accounts. I'd have to go see. I don't know."

"This the capitalist society. Now you see why we don't want it," she muttered. "No responsibility. Me first."

"You abandon your children too," I said defensively, trying to better my position.

"That's true," she said matter-of-factly. "But we clear. The children we keep, we die for."

Chiong kept about the business of the house, and whatever sanity reigned was entirely due to her kind concern.

But no matter what she did, and she did try, she could not budge me. I didn't bathe. I didn't wash my hair or teeth. I fell into a ragamuffin, yes, homeless-child lethargy that threatened to engulf me.

I ate so little that by the end of the second week I had lost ten pounds. It was because of this weight loss that the press later dubbed me anorexic. I'm not. Nor have I ever been. Which is solely because I trained at the feet of Dr. Manny Hart. One can overcome one's pathology with the right teacher. I know this.

I was afraid to tell anyone in authority that Fishbite was gone–Miss Manly, say, or Mr. Turkman–lest I end up in a foster home. I entertained the idea of asking Eglantine's mother to adopt me, but I was too embarrassed to do it. And I guess I still hoped, then, that he'd come back.

27 My lawyer, Ms. Velvet Glove, wants me to tell you how it really was with me deep down inside, away from all the glib phrases and humorous gibes.

It was so black I couldn't see. My head and heart stumbled around, bruising their delicate boundaries on unseen and treacherous corners until I was so sore inside my skin it hurt to move.

What I can bear to remember was outside myself. It was a week when several children were beaten to death, one was starved, and a newborn was abandoned in the bathroom at Tomorrowland—as if it would be better for the child to be abandoned there than anywhere else—as if somehow when the child looked back, it could look on that with pride.

I somehow got through the anguish of that first week and then, on the Wednesday of the second week, I became furious. It happened in a second—a rage blew up in me when I awoke and I started spitting glass.

First, I went into the bedroom where we had slept and took a firewood ax to the Chinese wedding bed. The sound of my hacking reverberated down the halls of the empty house.

"What are you doing?" Chiong asked when she arrived for work. She stood in the doorway with a worried look.

I smashed the ax over and over into the ornate, carved teakwood, but I was not actually strong enough to do much more than nicking damage.

"I am making meaning," I told her, and she nodded and walked away, down the stairs to the kitchen.

I had not as yet entered Fishbite's old office. But now, enraged, I got the key from a kitchen drawer and ran down the front steps and let myself in.

It was dusty in the rooms but warm, messy in that indiscriminate way it is when people move out, and empty. An old button lay here, a film canister lid there, a single sock left behind with a bit of crumpled up paper. The rolltop desk was still there; I could see it from the doorway.

For several days I could not enter his writing room. I sat in the doorway and wondered what I had done. Had he become too afraid of discovery? Was it the playlet and the sight of the police that made him run? Why didn't he tell me? Why didn't he say good-bye?

Why didn't he make sure I would be all right? Why didn't he help me? Couldn't he just call?

I ranged around the front room of the downstairs apartment breaking the mirror on a closet door, slicing up the sofa cushion with a kitchen knife and dragging out the stuffing, toppling the side tables, and upsetting the lamps. But still I could not enter his office.

In the afternoons, I went out. I had found twenty dollars in a coat pocket and I now went off to McDonald's for one meal a day. But I had some trouble there. If the clerk mistook my order or something somehow was wrong, I went berserk. The rabid ferret girl in me mounted the counter and leaped onto the shirtfront of the unsuspecting worker. I no longer cared how much I hurt these unknown people. I had no sense of them as living beings. If you ask me, as a talk-show host might, how I felt just then, it was as if I was hiccuping hate.

On one of these forays, I went by Evie Naif's building and chatted up the day doorman. The Naifs were on vacation, he told me, the parents to Gstaad, Evie to Disney World. No one was staying in their apartment. They would not be back home for another two weeks.

To make sure that Fishbite was not in their building, I befriended the maintenance man and gave him some very old brandy as a bribe to enter their place. No one was at the Naifs' now, nor had been for at least two to three weeks, he reported. It gave me one surge of pleasure to think that in his haste, Fishbite had run out on Evie, too.

I was glad the sex was done, so glad. I was no longer doing wrong and I was so relieved. It was like a heavy old grown-up's overcoat had been taken off my little shoulders. I felt like Amahl when Jesus heals him and he throws away his crutch and dances. It took me about a minute to revert back to my baby self and to close up that door forever.

I vowed that no one would ever know that anything different had happened to me. I would never tell anyone because, as my mother used to say, "Never tell what you don't want people to know, Lucky. You tellin' someone is how they find out."

I felt that if nobody knew and no one reminded me and I never thought about it, it would be as if it never happened. And maybe that would have been true, had I not found Fishbite's diary.

And even after the unpleasantness, it was my lawyer, Ms. Glove, who insisted on the abuse defense. As the CEO of WHINE!, I would never have condoned that—but she convinced me. My work in the future was what made me go for it. And that it generally publicized the abuse of children.

But the tricky part of all of it was that I was not just a child abused by this time, I was also a woman scorned, and from both sides of my brain, I felt awful about it.

28

I entered Fishbite's writing room finally on my hands and knees. I crawled in, pushing my whole body through the fear, butting it with my head.

The floor smelled dusty and woody and the cold winter light of a cloudy day shone through the bank of windows and illuminated my path. Slowly, doggedly, I crawled toward the rolltop desk, past wads of crumpled-up novel, past dried-up ballpoints, past intricate dust balls of hair and string. How do those things get made? I wondered as I passed them on my way to the wall of wooden drawers that was his desk. Spontaneous generation?

I sat before this holy relic of his presence on my knees, as befitted a geisha. One by one, I pulled out the drawers, searching intently for some solace for my plight.

Nothing here. Nothing there. A rubber band. A paper clip. A receipt from the Ten Freedoms Spa in Chinatown. I vowed to go there but never did. Ah, here, one sepia copy of a daguerreotype. A Lewis Carroll. And there is Alice, looking cowed and vacant—how I know that look! I'd never seen that photo before. He'd shown me others far less damning.

The left-hand drawer was still locked. I got up and rushed to the outer room to find my ax. When I ran back, I swung it at the drawer and broke the front of it up. Inside the broken slats lay something precious that he'd forgot. The antique gun that Vanda gave him. He must have moved it there, the tiny pearl-handled revolver, the gun a child could shoot, and shortly would.

I took it out carefully and looked for bullets but it was unloaded and I found none. I set the gun on top of the desk and continued my search. Nothing more. Nothing was there.

I set the gun over by the bank of windows on the floor and took my ax to the desk. I hit it and hit it, with such force finally that it moved and I heard something that had been wedged behind it fall and hit the floor behind.

I peered over to investigate and saw, to my amazement, that what had fallen on the floor was Fishbite's diary. Somehow it had fallen behind the desk and he'd forgotten it. Or maybe he'd left it for me to finish. I'd never know for sure.

I took it up and sat down in the swivel chair and began to read the truth.

29

It is rare that a child gets to read what grown-ups really think, and good thing, too. It nearly killed me. Many times I had to stop and wipe my eyes. I wept not rivers but cascades of tears to learn what somewhere deep inside I sensed.

Dear Readers and Watchers, he never loved me. Love wasn't written there. Lust, desire, obsession, yes, but never love. Of course I knew it all along, but still you hope, you know, you hope.

It was he who killed my mother. First he tried to drown her in Greece, then he pushed her off the roof, and then—page 200, bottom:

It took a while to get the taxi license but I got it. Courtesy that fella Cloaka's i.d. which he left behind in the desk. Of course he had a chauffeur's license, all con men do if they are worth a damn.

It was pitiable how simple it was to run her over. It's hard to believe I just parked outside Boxer Rebellion and shouted her name and that's all it took. I guess I won't forget how she came running to see what was up when she saw me at the wheel of a taxi. I don't actually remember running up onto the sidewalk and over the woman. No point in it. She never knew what hit her. I don't aim to inflict needless suffering.

Some angel was watching over me because I got away with everyone watching. And it was strange—those damn little shoes all over the cab, their sharp little toes pointing at me. I threw them in the first trashbin I found on the turnpike, where I raced to get clear of the whole damn business. I have to tell Lucky some story when I get her from Chutney but all I can think about is—she's mine. The adorable little creature is mine!

It was all there, how he picked me up, how he dragged me off to Lake Innuendo because of an ad in a girlie magazine, how he broke the news in that German diner in front of that old, old lady.

For a while, I could not read about the sex. I was too scared. I walked around the empty room and stared out into the garden. I tried to ready myself for what was to come, but I never could have foreseen it.

Page 220:

Oral sex. Only oral sex. She is one controlling little lady. She forced me to visit Evie. Odd coincidence—little Evie doing a shoot here. She is hot as a pistol. Left Lucky and went to her room, and one-two-three, we were at it like rabbits. That child is not a virgin, which shocks me, and only eleven.

30

It was all there, Dear Readers and Watchers, their whole tawdry affair, the answers to any questions I might have had, any absences I might have wondered about. He had not shown respect, as I had thought, or sexual restraint; the whole time he was interfering with Evie Naif.

I took the pearl-handled pistol off the desk top and put it in my pocket. I now knew where Fishbite was. The question was what hotel was he staying at. Stuck into the diary was a brochure that told the story: "A Vacation the Children Will Always Remember! The Puffin Hotel in Disney World!"

31

Chiong had found some of my mother's credit cards when she was cleaning, in an old silk purse at the back of her closet. After washing myself and dressing like a rich Hatpin girl, I used the cards to limo to the airport and purchase my ticket to Orlando, Florida.

While I waited for the plane, I unfortunately passed a newsstand. There on the cover of a daily was a mother's boyfriend's description of suffocating her child. "I taped her mouth and when she stopped squeezing my hand, I knew she was dead," it quoted the animal. The child had defended the mother when he and the mother fought. Death was the child's reward.

Before I could stop myself, I turned on the newsstand owner. "Don't you understand," I screamed. "Only people who don't care can read this filth. She trusted her mother!"

In a rage, I swept all the papers off their shelves onto the airport carpeting. Then, realizing what I had done, I ran and hid in one of the ladies' rooms. I stood by the door, and when I heard my flight called, I dashed toward the security machines.

I removed from my backpack a small, old leather gun-case, which I handed to the security lady.

"It's an old pearl-handle revolver," I said. "Unloaded. I'm bringing it down to my grandmother for her collection. She has a small museum." I smiled innocently.

The security lady looked confused.

"Here's my proof of purchase," I handed her the papers. "Here's my license from the Firearms Control Board. Here's my airline permission."

She examined the papers.

"You are eighteen?" she asked me.

"Yes," I replied as pleasantly as I could.

"Okay," she said. "Walk through."

I set off no buzzers. I had no bullets on me. I would buy them as soon as I got off in Florida. I had gotten my contra- band papers through Evie's doorman, a fact that will always delight me.

The security lady handed me the leather case and I returned it to my backpack. Three hours later, I was in Orlando.

I hitched a ride to the hotel with a Japanese businessman who tried to kiss me several times but who was good-natured when I pushed him away.

I did let him feel my breast in return for buying me some bullets, though. I squeezed up my eyes like I do when I take bitter medicine and I hardly felt him touch me. Then we just pulled up to a gun shop and he got out and bought bullets for me and brought them back to the car. I took the package, transferred to the front seat, and rode with the driver to my hotel.

32

The Puffin was a strange place. Designed by a famous and clearly frustrated architect, it was a big hotel of smooth red stone flanked by two turrets, atop which were two giant Atlantic puffins.

On the grounds was a canal that led to the Magic Kingdom, a white sand beach with a playground on it, five swimming pools, including two kiddie pools, and supremely manicured lawns where puffins roosted and waddled.

The lobby was grand and spotless and in its center was a fountain decorated with mechanical puffins who swooped and caught fake fish in their orange-and-red beaks.

I checked in with my mother's credit card and at the same time inquired about Evie.

"What room is Evie Naif in? I'm with the same modeling agency. We're meeting to go to Disney World. I can hardly wait!"

I leaped up and down and reverted to childhood for a moment. I did used to like Mickey Mouse a long time ago, back in Texas. I had a Mickey that I clutched whenever Tex left the house.

"My Mickey," I would yell as he closed the door and my mother would bring it to me.

I used it as a talisman to make sure he would come back, but when he didn't, I gave it up. I took it from the suitcase when my mother was packing to leave the state, and threw it in a corner. This was the first time I'd thought of Mickey since then.

"Evie and I are going to meet Mickey!" I told the registration clerk. "My dad's arriving this afternoon."

The woman smiled as she looked up Evie's room. Her eyebrows furrowed. "No Naif," she said. "Another name, perhaps?"

"Fishbite," I said. "Roger Fishbite." She adjusted her computer and then smiled.

"Room 202," she said. "Let's put you in 204. Should I phone your friend?"

"Oh no! Let me surprise her, please," I begged, and she laughed.

I ran off to the elevators and took one to the second floor. I let myself into 204 and then peeked back out at the hallway. All was silent. The hallway was white but painted with murals of puffins heading for the sea. I didn't like looking at them. They disturbed me. I closed the door.

I lay down on the bed and fell asleep. It was after lunch when I was awakened. The maids were entering the room.

I said hello and popped out into the hall to see if the door to Evie's room stood open. It did. The big cart with sheets and towels was parked outside. I darted into her room and looked around.

Fishbite was definitely here. Here was his briefcase, his clothes, his disguises. All strewn around and entangled with her little designer frocks. All the little shoes she'd brought with her, all ten pairs, were lined up on the window sill next to each other. I spit in each pair because I could not help myself. Then I hid in the closet.

After the maids had left I propped open the door and went into my room to get the gun. I took it from my backpack, loaded it, and returned to Evie's room to wait.

33

Here at the facility, I'm a bit of a celebrity to the other girls. I am the first sexually abused girl-child (that I've heard of in the media) to actually murder her abuser. Most children "displace," I think they call it in psychology. They hurt other people or animals or themselves. But that was not for me.

Not that I deserve any credit, really. It was Evie I thought I wanted to kill. But when I got into their room and saw that he had rumpled up the beds to make it look as if they'd slept in both–just like he used to do with me–I realized she was just a pawn too. I got so angry that when I heard the key card in the door, I stood right in front of it, pointing the gun with my two hands around the grip, the way policewomen do on TV.

And suddenly there he was. And the rabid ferret girl leaped out of my chest, looked into his eyes, and fired. The bullet went right over Evie's head. She was standing in front of him. She'd entered first, though I didn't see her. I was looking at his face. It got him in the heart.

"Lucky," he gasped as he pitched forward. Evie scooted out of the way.

I looked down at him. He was huge. He lay at my feet like a dead elephant I saw once on a show about poachers in a game park.

In an instant, it seemed, Evie, bless her heart, had managed to pack her things. Barbie hatbox in one hand and signature parasol in the other, she now squeezed by us.

"I like you," she told me as she carefully stepped over the gasping Fishbite and opened the door. "Let's have a playdate sometime." And out she fled into the corridor.

"Lucky?" a voice gurgled.

Fishbite, it appeared, was not yet dead.

Suddenly I was scared of what I'd done. I started shaking all over. He was bleeding profusely, the energy visibly ebbing out of his great prone form, the blood seeping over one of his well-thumbed paperbacks. "Lucky," he gurgled again.

"What?" I asked him, backing away toward the door. I was afraid he would grab my legs and pull me down. I began to sob uncontrollably.

"It wasn't her, baby. I was scared," he whispered. "Call an ambulance—we'll stay together . . ."

"No," I told him, taking his diary from my pocket and throwing it onto his body. "No, I can't. I know everything now."

His eyes glanced at the diary, which had dropped down against his cheek. "Uh-oh" was all he said before he died.

34

Ms. Glove, my lawyer, asked me to make sure you understand that when I went to the Magic Kingdom right after this, I was out of my mind. I don't remember all the details. I do remember the sun spraying across the fishless man-made canal. One hundred Pluto dogs staring at me from the window of a shop on Main Street. And Mickey and Minnie doing a dance number in front of the enchanted castle that included the American flag.

I remember wishing that I had someone to love me and that there wasn't so much violence and that I'd get my own show. And I remember seeing Fishbite's face and my mother's on Goofy and Snow White and all the little Thai-landers as dwarfs. Pinocchio was Tex, and when he approached me, his white-gloved hand extended, I screamed and ran and ended up in the bathroom at Tomorrow-land, where I crouched against the ugly gray concrete and wept.

And then, after what seemed an eternity, I stood up and washed my hands and face and then lay down on the floor of a stall and waited.

I mistook the Disney World security for midwives when they came. But I was not wrong in thinking that somehow they'd deliver me.

Chicago, Illinois
June 1998

When I went to meet Lucky Linderhof at the Flanders Juvenile Corrections Facility in the fall of 1996, I assumed she was just another thirteen-year-old child murderess with a knack for publicity. By then, I'd had my talk show for ten years. In my business, you see everything, twice.

But I'd never seen anyone like little Lucky. Beautiful, articulate, well-bred, educated, socially responsible, she was exactly what the public does not associate with sexual abuse, drunkenness, con games, and murder.

My producers (and you can't blame them—they are in business; I'm the one in caring), they called her a gold mine, and I could not disagree. I mean, this was a child who was not only working on a tie-in memoir but had an idea for her own show and a social agenda to go with it.

When she told us about her show, *Babytalk*, and her organization, WHINE!, and what she wanted to do with it all, we just looked at each other and said, "Girlfriends, we got to go back and take a production meeting."

And, of course, as the world knows, because she is one of the most requested interviews in *People* magazine's history, her show goes on from the facility where she is incarcerated, beginning this September, weekdays at four P.M. so the kids can watch when they are back from school.

And people have asked me, "Warma, is she for real or is she just a clever killer?"

And what I say to them and you is this: The jury found her guilty of second-degree murder, which makes her a killer. During the trial, her news conferences on the plight of children raised ten million dollars for global children's charities, including her own (WHINE!), and completely bankrupted the Pike's Peak sneaker company, which makes her very clever. And she carries in her purse a little ragged piece of her infant blanket, which she calls Peco, and which, when I see her with it, makes me feel she is very real.

See for yourself. Weekdays at four. Starting in September.

Warma Moneytree
Star of *The Warma Moneytree Show*
Executive Producer of *Babytalk*

Author's Note

This novel is in part a literary parody of that great work *Lolita* by Vladimir Nabokov. It is my reply both to the book and to the icon that the character Lolita has become.

ABOUT THE AUTHOR

EMILY PRAGER is the author of *A Visit from the Footbinder and Other Stories* and the novels *Clea and Zeus Divorce* and *Eve's Tattoo*. She began her writing career at the *National Lampoon* magazine and has written humor for major magazines, as well as political satire columns for the *New York Observer, The Village Voice,* and *The New York Times.* She lives in New York City with her daughter.

ABOUT THE TYPE

This book was set in Walbaum, a typeface designed in 1810 by German punch cutter J. E. Walbaum. Walbaum's type is more French than German in appearance. Like Bodoni, it is a classical typeface, yet its openness and slight irregularities give it a human, romantic quality.